Passion Within: When Our Love Met

By Milan

Published by PageFree Publishing, Inc. 2002
ISBN 1-930252-83-8

Republished in 2003 by:
Ronnie Boodoo, Inc.
801 Lancaster Street
Baltimore, MD 21202

ISBN 0-9728029-1-6

A Dedication to the Special People Who Molded My Life

I dedicate this work to:

Joshua and Glendalin Cane,

Joseph Mason,

Debbie Sanders,

Ronald Boodoo,

Jackie Miller,

Mr. Ray Martin and all my teachers who educated me to be the person I am today,

and those who supported me in all that I did.

Above all, I dedicate this work to the readers who support this work.

Part One
Birthing His Love

When a man beholds true love in you
He'll do his best to find his way through
To win your hand no matter the wait
He will tempt the very fiber of fate

One

She stepped into a place so lush
Where butterflies carried on in no rush
And sat in a rainbow of flowers
As dew fell from the trees in showers

Her hair rested around her neck and back
While squirrels ate from her barley sack
And birds descended to her gentle hand
As her feet touched and blessed this lush land

Her refreshing smile competed with the sun
Yet her enchanting spell had just begun
To capture souls with her sparkling eyes
Would loving her be my demise?

That is impossible to be
For inside her there is beauty
In her there is passion desired
In this garden she inspired

Adding to a smile that blessed for hours
Is her presence surrounded by flowers
In this garden of divine beauty

And without her, none of this could be.

"Stop dreaming, Romelus; she belongs to Titus," came the high-pitched sound of Kimbi's voice. He was a young clown and Romelus's best friend. His pale skin, beaten under the blistering sun, glistened with sweat as he made his way over to Romelus.

"It is a shame that our words of poetry and satire are used to entertain, yet our gifts are considered necessary evil," Romelus remarked, not shifting his gaze from the alluring young woman in the garden below. His dark skin also glistened with sweat from the radiant heat of the sun as he brushed his long, wavy hair from his dark-brown eyes and pulled it around his ear so it hung comfortably over his shoulders. His slender frame propped lazily against a boulder while his parchment lay against his lap with a few other scrolls leaning against the boulder beside him.

"Well at least we performers can read and write." Kimbi slumped beside Romelus and snatched the parchment from him. He looked over the poem and said compassionately—and then teased, "Rome, this is very good, but I hope you do not intend to barter your life for this girl; she is our master's wife___ What about that woman who came with one of master's guests last night?" Romelus looked puzzled, his mind searching for a memory of last night's event.

"I don't know what you are talking about my friend; I stole some wine not yet diluted in water and got drunker than Titus himself," he replied, taking back his parchment and setting it down with the others on the ground beside him.

"Well let me tell you___ You two were all over each other under the coliseum while the gladiators fought. She was a pretty one you lucky dog," Romelus looked puzzled, listening to his friend ramble, "Don't you remember me taking you back to your quarters?" Kimbi informed roguishly as he punched Romelus on the arm.

Romelus looked at his friend, whose smile was contagious and caused him to smile as well while repeating, "I do not remember." He rubbed his arm where Kimbi punched him and adjusted himself to a more comfortable position.

They lay against the lush earth, silently looking out at the garden below, with the sun shining brightly and silver clouds decorating the sky. Birds filled the air with a myriad of colors, adding life to an endless blue sky that kissed the green trees at the horizon while shadows danced to the rhythm of the warm breeze that combed gently through the nearby trees.

"Pray man; tell me___ what is her name? For I must know," Romelus whispered to his friend, breaking the silence of serenity.

Kimbi rolled his eyes. "Not this again; well, if you must know… her name is a bit long to pronounce, but I have heard master call her Nikkia." He stood to his feet and started walking away. "I have to prepare my performance for master's feast and it is not as easy as learning poetry. So Rome___ when you come down from your dream world with master's wife in it, I hope you have time to do your work." He disappeared over the hill behind Romelus.

"Her flowing hair seems to frolic to heavenly music against the

wind___ and her blue eyes: so enchanting. Her body appears to move with the grace of a goddess from a distant land. Her dance of seduction sends chills over my body with every motion. The danger of death is upon me for what I am about to do," Romelus thought to himself as he stood and made his way between the flowerbeds and ponds towards Nikkia. "Good day Mistress. It is an exceptionally delightful day with you in it," he greeted as he bowed before her.

Her brilliant smile captured the moment when she turned and bowed. "I see___ the poet Romelus. I want to thank you for your recital at my wedding which you performed so eloquently," inviting him to sit at a nearby bench. To him, her blue eyes sparkled like a still, blue ocean under the incandescently sunlit sky, and her ever-present smile was like a warm summer's breeze on a cold winter's night as she spoke to him.

"I have written another just inspired; would you like to read it?" Romelus pulled the parchment from his pile and handed it to her. "It was inspired by this garden; master Titus lets us roam in the afternoon to prepare for his lavish events," he finally spoke, after admiring her statuesque beauty with an inducing smile. He was still afraid of her because she had the power to end his life, but he was compelled to express himself honestly.

She pushed the parchment back to him apologizing, "Forgive me poet for not reading your poem; I cannot read the text. Is that Latin or Greek?"

Romelus took the parchment without altering his gaze from her gorgeous face in contrition. "Forgive me mistress, I did not realize…

because you speak Latin so well. I forgot you are from Gaul and that you may not have gotten the opportunity to learn to read this text." She smiled at him and he looked away nervously. "To answer your question, this poem is in Latin, which I can teach you if you like." He looked, once again, into her enchanting eyes as her pale skin, tanned from the sun's rays, added brilliance to her blue orbs.

"I would love that, poet; we can meet under that tree in the meadow tomorrow." She pointed to a tree in the distance. "Under that tree." And then she leaned over to look at the parchment. Romelus read slowly, articulating and pointing to every word so she would understand and see what he was reading. Her gentle signs of appreciation encouraged him, through the poem, to reach into the abyss of his being and pour out the quiddity of his soul.

They conversed into the early evening. Romelus learned how Titus wanted her, so he settled a debt that her father owed in exchange for her hand in marriage. She agreed to the marriage in obedience to her father's command and to keep her family safe from Titus's wrath, forTitus was an influential man in Caesar's court. Her courage and virtue astonished him as he listened. He parted for the night, clasping his poem in his hand with much zeal stating, "This will be called *A Beautiful Garden*."

Two

The sun rose over the horizon on its journey across the land with Romelus already up and working diligently on trans-scripting books for Titus's library. The cool morning breeze blew across his naked back sending chills along his spine as the door to his dwelling flew open. Titus walked in, adorned in his toga made from Asian silk. His weather-beaten face had a stern expression as he strolled confidently into the room, his body still in excellent condition considering his frequent events filled with eating and drinking.

Romelus quickly rose from his seat to greet his master. "Good morning, master. What service do you request of me?" He bowed. Titus walked around the room looking at his slave's work.

"This seems to be coming along nicely, but I have another request for you___ a job that must be done if you value your life, slave." He paused and took a few more steps. "Caesar will be here tomorrow and there will be a feast in his honor. You are to recite for us; then___ by Brutus' command, you are to fight in the gladiator's pit." He turned and looked at Romelus, whose eyes focused on the ground at his feet.

"Yes, master," he answered feeling as though he was about to die. He knew it would be fruitless to defy Titus's command, even more so since the request came from Brutus.

Titus walked to the door and then stopped. "My wife asked if you could teach her to read Latin." He chuckled. "I told her yes___ only if you survive tomorrow night." He turned, roaring out cynically, laughing and muttering to himself, "We shall see if a poet can fight as good as he writes." He disappeared out of sight and Romelus fell to his knees overwhelmed by sorrow.

Romelus picked himself up after a while to finish his work, and then he grabbed some parchments and made his way out to the garden. He lumbered through the garden thinking of the event of his death when a familiar voice broke the silence of his thoughts. "Why the long face my friend!?" Kimbi ran up to him.

Romelus replied so depressingly that he could put a dog's howl at the moon to shame, "Oh! My life is about to end___ I will surely die tomorrow."

Kimbi looked a little puzzled and asked as he slapped Romelus on his back, causing him to stumble, "Why do you say that?" They walked on as Kimbi waited for his friend to speak.

"Caesar will be here tomorrow and requested that I recite—." He paused while Kimbi laughed hysterically, taunting Romelus, who did not crack a smile.

"Since when does death come from speaking?" Kimbi agitated Romelus after his roll of laughter ended.

Romelus looked into his eyes. "It is not the recital___ I am to also stand my own in the gladiator's pit." Kimbi's joyous face lengthened into serious solitude. They meandered in silence through the garden for a short while before Romelus turned to his friend, breaking the ghostly silence suggesting, "Kimbi, can you teach me to fight? I am in excellent shape from running around with master, carrying those parchments from village to village, and from carrying water. I may not be as big as you, but I am faster than you are."

Kimbi looked at his friend and cracked his usually mischievous smile. "Much of my satire does lead to battle, but those are played out before-hand, my friend___ To learn from me is to surely die." He hugged Romelus and wished him good luck before disappearing back to the slaves' dwelling area and to his work.

Three

The evening drew near, and Romelus walked towards the meadow where he planned to meet Nikkia as promised the night before. The verdurous green grass sprouted towards the sky while sheep grazed on it, denying it from reaching its goal. The tree stood in the distance upon a small hill where they planned to meet. Blossoms of white and pink flowers decorated the tree as it complimented the llano green meadow below it. He caught a movement from behind the tree and realized it was Nikkia, looking lovelier than the day before. He stopped in his tracks, admiring her ardently as he sat, missing the rock he was aiming for, making the soft grass his seat. Her presence seemed to lift the danger of death from his heart as she moved mellifluously around, plucking blossoms from the tree and catching whiffs of their pleasing fragrance before releasing them into the caring embrace of the gentle wind. Romelus quickly opened a parchment, and with a burst of vigor, started to write:

A Beautiful Scene

Out on the meadow in flowing white
Her beauty compliments this gorgeous sight
Her graceful stride so angelic sweet
As I sat, I missed my seat

The colors of blossoms all around

Is not as pleasant as her smile or frown
The tree seems to bow as she pass it by
While the sun shines brighter in the sky

The green grass softens at her touch
That there's no other scene as such
The gold that she wears on her skin
Enhances her beauty that makes my head spin

As the sun reflects off her gorgeous eyes
So ocean blue as they hypnotize
The birds in the tree sing out from their hearts
While mine has been singing from the start

All of nature seems to worship her
An entrancing woman who Heaven stirred
For when she walks away from sight
I'll remember her this way on this night.

"Good evening, Mistress___ I hope you slept well," Romelus kowtowed, after dashing up the hill towards Nikkia.

"Hello, Romelus. Are you ready to teach me Latin?"

He rose from his bow. "Yes, mistres; I am ready." He opened his parchments after they sat at the base of the tree—Nikkia waited patiently.

"Romelus, you do not have to call me mistress all the time. I am as much in bondage as you are; so please call me Nikkia," she demanded of him over the crackle of the parchment.

He acknowledged her request, and then he turned looking into her eyes saying, "I may not be here to teach you after tomorrow night, Nikkia; as you well know, I will be fighting for my life in the pit."

She solemnly looked away into the distance. "I know, poet… so I brought you a gift… I hope this will help you tomorrow." She pulled a cloth riddled with spikes from a pouch lying beside her. "My brother hunted beasts for the coliseum games and showed me once, before he died, how he caught lions; he used a cloth like this with the spikes stained with a sleeping poison. When the creature leapt at him, he would move to one side, wrapping the cloth around its neck, letting the poison do its work. I hope you are successful tomorrow."

He took the cloth, offering his gratitude to her. He looked at the fabric for a while and then turned to her asking, "Am I to fight a lion tomorrow?"

"Yes___ you will be fighting Tetros. I've heard he is the most vicious of Titus's beasts… so be careful." He could hear the softness in her voice that seemed to comfort him.

He looked at the cloth again, and then wrapped it carefully before placing it beside him. "Thank you, Nikkia; I hope I live tomorrow to thank you again."

The sun descended slowly over the hilltop as Romelus taught letters to Nikkia. His patience was astounding when frustration blanketed her mind. After the lesson was over, he opened his parchment of the poem he wrote earlier. "Just in case death greets me tomorrow, I want you to know I wrote a poem inspired by you while you were walking earlier___ so was the one I read to you yesterday. Would you like to hear it?"

A tranquil smile covered his face as she looked at the parchment and replied, "I would love to hear it, and hopefully, it would not be the last." He read his poem with all his heart, breaking the boundaries of passionate expression, before ending in silent tears as she looked affectionately into his glassy eyes.

"That was beautiful, and it was even more special because it is about me," she complimented while he rolled his parchment close.

"I will be reciting this poem tomorrow." He stood to his feet. "Well, Nikkia, the night is almost upon us. Practice those letters, and day after tomorrow… we will meet again to continue your lesson. Thanks again for the cloth," taking her hand and kissing it—never breaking eye contact. His affection for her multiplied upon receiving her gift, a gift he knew she did not have to give, but she gave it selflessly. He did not think it would work since he knew the power of a lion and thought her brother was only shielding her from the actual danger he faced in capturing beasts for the coliseum. But she believed that it could work.

"Good night, Romelus. I will stay here for a bit, for the sky is beautiful and reminds me of home… the duties of Titus's wife is taxing, but at least here I can have some peace." He bowed, before taking his leave for the night.

Four

Caesar's chariot trotted towards Titus's dwelling with his slave at the reins. His armor shone brightly in the evening sun as his host of soldiers, dressed according to their rank, brought up the rear. His sword hung around his lower tunic while his shield lined the space between his foot and the inner chariot wall. His rigid expression of focus preceded him as they made their way towards Titus's country dwelling. Brutus rode expertly beside Caesar on his silver horse and his muscles flexed with every bounce, controlling his swift steed. His stoic expression, with a hint of a smirk, demanded respect as he proudly maneuvered his horse. They came to a halt at Titus's dwelling, meeting their host with Nikkia at his side, while Titus's most attractive slaves waited nearby, ready to escort his guests. Titus stepped forward and greeted Caesar with a smile while slaves came forth to steady the animals as the soldiers came to a halt.

"Welcome___ welcome," Titus happily greeted.

Brutus kicked the slave who tried to assist him and dismounted with nothing short of grace while shouting harshly, "Don't touch my horse you filthy animal!" The slave rose to his feet and took the reins, and he guided the animal to the stable.

Caesar's stern face relaxed into a homely smile when he greeted Titus as his Generals dismounted, and then he looked at Nikkia with an even wider grin. "Is this your wife?" he asked Titus, as he took her hand. Titus nodded his answer as she bowed before Caesar who lifted her upright looking her over. He turned to Titus saying jokingly for all to hear, "If I had known how beautiful she was___ by Jupiter___ I would have married her myself!" They laughed at the joke and were guided by the slaves into the atrium.

Beautiful slaves bustled around with trays of fresh fruit and watered down wine, while others fanned certain guests. Many performances unfolded for Titus and his guests into the early night while they indulged in the wine and the women who served them.

From the roar of laughter and merriment, Caesar shouted out, "Where is that linguist slave of yours Titus!?" Romelus stood and took his position, and the room silenced to a muffle.

"Recite boy—first in Latin, and then in Greek!" Titus bellowed, almost intoxicated. Romelus obeyed and recited in the order Titus commanded, and then he took his bow deliberately keeping his gaze away from Nikkia, for fear of agitating his master.

Nikkia looked at him, suppressing the tears that swelled in her eyes, as Romelus poured out his heart. She heaved with every gesture knowing that every word spoken was inspired by her. Brutus noticed her expressions that she failed to suppress and leaned over to Titus saying insinuatingly, "That slave of yours has a way with words… he must also have a way with women too."

He gestured to Nikkia, who heard the venomous words spoken, and roguishly responded, "His words do possess a certain power, but in the end he is still a slave used for entertainment and nothing more than that." Her denouement seemed to soften Titus's jealousy that Brutus managed to sow in his heart, so the festivities continued with the chaotic comment soon forgotten.

The party shifted into Titus's private coliseum already lit for the night's event. It was a modest size since it was constructed for private use. Although the audience was near the action, they were elevated out of harm's way.

"Bring in that slave!" Brutus shouted to one of his legionaries. They dragged in a woman dressed in rags, and although she kicked and screamed, it was no use. Her bare feet pounded against the stone floor as she continued to struggle. At the opposite end of the coliseum, two legionaries pushed a couple of slaves carrying a cross into the middle of the arena to hasten their pace while another two soldiers made their way to the cross. The two legionaries, who dragged the enceinte woman, punched and battered her into a silent sob as they dragged her into the light, revealing her swollen womb while still trouncing her stomach. Nikkia gasped at the sight but said nothing. The slave forced with all her might—sending her screams into the night. Nikkia watched in agony, but there was nothing she could do, for Titus was lord and master of all his holdings and his wrath could weigh heavily upon her. A tear hung from her eye-lid as she tried to suppress the quivering rage in her heart. The slave screamed to the point of hoarseness while the legionaries, who met the slaves with the cross at the center of the coliseum, revealed spikes and a hammer: preparing for the crucifixion. They first strapped her to the cross before the two legionaries who brought her in were dismissed. The spike driver and his younger companion remained.

"Drive the stake!" Brutus shouted to the men below. The older soldier held a spike over one of the slave's forearms while the younger soldier held her down to minimize movement.

She looked into the spike driver's eyes, pleading through sorrowful sobs, "Please…(sob) don't do th… this___ My baby was my only crime; if you let me go…(sob) I will leave this place and raise my baby where Brutus…(sniff) could never hurt it…(sob) He is doing this because he does not want this child."

Her tears gushed like a raging river down her cheeks as the legionary looked into her eyes, clemently saying, "Forgive me." He knew to disobey an imperial command would be certain death.

He drove the spike into her as she shrieked out in pain. The sound of the hammer against the spike changed tone, transfixing into the cross. Her eyes shot tightly with pain wrenching her body as the legionary moved quickly to her other hand, delivering the same blow: driving the second spike. The blood poured from her veins as her rounded stomach bounced against the cross's beam. He drove the last spike through both her feet with swift precision, suppressing the hurt he felt. The shocking pain countered with adrenaline worked slowly on her body as enraged slaves hoisted her into the air—unable to do anything but watch and obey, for fear of suffering the same fate.

The two legionaries walked away when the younger one asked his colleague, "Why did you ask that slave for forgiveness? We are superior to them."

The older man looked at his young companion with a stern expression and replied, "We are not immune to the crucifixion ourselves; you will soon learn about that. We fight for Rome and the glory of Caesar, but to take a helpless life, and in this case two, is to live a lifetime of torment. For what we just did was the taking of a life in cold blood—." His voice trailed as they disappeared from sight.

Five

The gladiators made their way into the coliseum with raging hearts for the crime committed against the pregnant slave. They fought each other to the death—some fighting men and others fighting wild beasts. The stench of blood filled the air as the victor of each battle stepped away from his lifeless opponent to receive Caesar's blessings while those who fought wild beasts and won were chosen to fight at the coliseum in Rome for the amusement of the public.

Romelus stood with the thoughts of the slave who hung from the cross as he watched a young gladiator being ripped to shreds by a hungry leopard. His cry shattered Romelus's thought, and the young gladiator's life left his body, leaving the leopard gnawing on his bones. After the attendants removed the beast from the coliseum and the remains of the gladiator were scrapped from the earth, a soldier pushed Romelus onto the dirt. Romelus's sword reflected the orange glow from the torches that lit the coliseum as he nervously walked onto the blood covered ground; the thought of a model slave about to fight for his life for the amusement of Caesar's court captured his mind without any signs of comfort. He stood facing the crucified woman—her blood slowly puddled at the base of the cross. His heart raced with fear of his own mortality, but he was soon distracted by the dragging sound of a gate rising at the other side of the coliseum. He plunged his sword into the earth before him while removing Nikkia's gift from his toga where he had it stored. Nikkia's instructions flooded his mind—he waited with anticipation. He had rethought his view on the cloth and felt that it might just save his life because the power of the animal against a sword would be too risky. He reasoned that he did not have anything to lose by taking a chance with the poisoned cloth.

"What is that slave of yours doing? Does he plan to cloth the beast?" Caesar asked, leaning over to Titus.

"He is a strange one, my liege, but an excellent slave."

The gate rose completely as eyes focused on it. A low growl came from the hole at the open gate like rolling thunder. It grew louder as the flash of yellow danced against the torches' light. The hungry lion walked slowly into the coliseum but quickly dropped into a stalker's crouch—the scent of blood tickling its nostrils. It reached the cross and circled it, licking the bloodstained stake. Romelus stood motionlessly as the lion ferociously slapped the dying slave's feet, sending needles of pain through her weak body. He watched, but made a grave mistake when he accidentally dragged his foot on the gravel to relieve the itch of an insect's bite. The beast turned its attention to the direction of the sound and saw a new prey in Romelus. It crouched low to the ground—its ears focused on him—it glided effortlessly, pausing after a few steps to assess its next move. Sweat streamed down Romelus's face, soaking the linen that wrapped his body when he again made a mistake by wiping the sweat from his face. Tetros saw this, and with nimble grace, silently leapt into the air with fire reflecting off its eyes. Romelus's life flashed before him as the lion extended its claws ready to shred its prey to pieces. The beast came down over him; Romelus lifted the cloth across its throat causing opposite forces to clash. The lion's downward force flipped Romelus onto its back, but Romelus held on to the cloth. He bounced off Tetros's back, and he was dragged around the coliseum as Tetros tried to remove the cloth that punctured its skin. The beast slashed and rolled, crushing Romelus under its weight for what seemed like an eternity, before finally slumbering to the ground. The fear in Romelus's eyes turned to relief as he stood to his feet; he still kept a watchful eye on the sleeping lion.

"That slave of yours would make an excellent gladiator," Caesar turned to Titus and commented almost completely drunk from the wine.

The crucified slave let out a whimper of pain—her head hung towards the earth. Romelus turned towards her; his expression changed from relief to compassion. He looked up at his audience and became enraged by their intoxicated merriment. He rushed for his sword in the dirt, drew it, and lunged towards the sleeping beast with a burst of energy. His audience turned their attention back to him as he approached Tetros. They leaned forward as he lifted the weapon above his head—light reflecting off the blade. He leaped into the air letting out a cry of rage and clearing Tetros. His audience then realized his target and watched in silence as his sword severed the bones and pierced the heart of the hanging slave, who managed a smile of thanks. Nikkia cried out in horror and dashed out of the room as the others watched, and then almost simultaneously, shouted out their praise for the added display of blood. The woman gave up the ghost almost immediately as Romelus fell to one knee on the ground before her, leaving the sword buried in her body and anchored in the cross.

Blood trickled from the new wound down her lifeless body to the earth before him as he knelt looking up at the starry sky. The country air blew into the coliseum, lifting the stench of blood, first around the coliseum, and then out into the bejeweled night. Slaves entered the coliseum and escorted Romelus to be cleaned while other slaves cautiously removed Tetros, for fear that it might awaken. They returned for the dead slave and her unborn child for burial that same night.

Six

Romelus raced up the hill towards the tree where Nikkia stood waiting for him. A joyous smile shined before him while the fresh breeze blew across his face, lifting his long curly hair off his shoulders. He reached Nikkia and noticed something was wrong. "Is everything okay?" He continued without waiting for an answer, "I really appreciate the advice and the gift you gave me; thank you." He finished as he rested his parchment at the tree trunk. Nikkia flared at him with rage in her eyes; her pale skin red with anger.

"What is the matter?" Romelus asked. He was confused at her angry tone.

She stepped to his face with fury and shouted, "I should have never shown you how to defeat Tetros, you heartless dog!" She turned away, but immediately turned back to him as he fell to his knees in fear. "I thought you were different___ kind and caring, but what you did last night was barbaric, far worst than any of the Germans!"

Romelus stood, now realizing the source of her anger towards him, and looked into her angry eyes, responding soothingly, "Would you like to know why I killed that slave last night? If I did not kill her, she would still be hanging there___ waiting for death to heal her pain. I have seen them hang for days before giving up the ghost and that was after their legs were broken." She looked into his eyes and saw a shimmer of suppressed tears, causing her to soften her expression and sat down, gesturing for him to do the same. He sat beside her. "Let me tell you about my childhood so you can understand a little better."

She sat silently waiting for him to speak. After a short pause, he opened his mouth and started: "My mother was the daughter of a Plebeian who traveled most of the year. I do not remember much about him, for I was very young when I was sold to slavery. My father, from what I was told, was sold into slavery to the Plebeian to be a gladiator, for he was strong and able for the sport. ___His mother was from India and his father was Egyptian, so his complexion was much like mine. That is all I know of my father and of what he looked like. He was sent back to Rome along with other cargo in the care of my mother. They fell in love somewhere on the journey, and I was conceived. My mother told me___ that was before we were separated___ that my father died on the journey saving our lives. A lion attacked her and he intervened. He killed the beast, but was badly injured and died shortly thereafter. Mother birthed me before we reached Rome, so a female slave who accompanied her took me as her own and raised me in secret with my mother once she returned here in Rome. She taught me Latin and Greek from the moment I started speaking___ that is why I am educated today. But the day came when my grandfather returned from his long expeditions in Africa. I made the grave mistake of entering the room where he and my mother conversed and called her *mother.* Usually I was kept in the slaves' quarters when my grandfather was at home, but this time no one knew of his arrival until it was too late. My grandfather was enraged, for he knew it had to be a slave, for I did not look like any Roman both dark or fair___ as you can see, my features are soft like that of the Asians. I watched him beat her into the ground…

spoiling her beautiful face for the disgrace she caused him. She was later disowned and sold into slavery because he did not have the heart to kill her. The last time I saw her, she was on her way to Egypt as a servant for a Roman General there. I often wonder at night how she's doing and if she is still alive," tears fell from his eyes, "My grandfather crucified every male slave who was his property for five years or more, and that is where I saw an image that caused me to release that slave last night from the torment she was going through. It was three days before the last slave died. Blood and tears stained the earth below where they hung while their agonizing cries filled the air, getting fainter and fainter as the blood left their veins. It is an image that will stay with me forever," she reached out and dried his cheek with her hair, "I can sometimes see it in my dreams at night, even though now it seems to be getting fainter. He kept me around for a few weeks before selling me to Titus___ and I have been here ever since. I am Roman in part, but it is the slave's blood that runs through my veins is what has damned me. So, when I killed that slave, it was to enable me to sleep better at night knowing that she is not still hanging on the cross suffering." Romelus fell silent while Nikkia dwelled on what he said. He dried his eyes and looked off into the distance.

She finally broke the silence and turned his stare to her, saying, "I am sorry, poet, for judging you so hastily; you showed mercy like the God of the Jews___ I have heard he had shown mercy much like what you have done." They conversed into the late evening before parting for the night.

Seven

Romelus and Nikkia met on the hill every day that she could make it, and her Latin greatly improved. The days turned to weeks and then months until one day she did not show. Romelus waited for her till the early evening, and thinking she may be occupied and unable to come, he left to return to his quarters. He took his usual walk through the garden with his parchments tucked under his arm, admiring the flowers and the pond as the fishes swam around. The serenity of the birds chirping and the setting sun in the distance in shades of orange and red distracted him until he heard a soft sobbing from behind a nearby flower hedge. He turned into the direction of the sound and rounded the corner of a hedge to reveal the source of the sobbing sound. Behold, before him Nikkia sat in tears with her hands covering her face. Romelus rushed up to her with concern flowing like a river from his face. He laid his parchment on the ground asking, "Why are you crying, Nikkia. Is there anything I can do?"

L…leave me be!" she exploded from behind her hands in a trembling voice.

He fell silent and sat beside her, patiently waiting, keeping her company. They sat there for what seemed like hours before Nikkia moved her hand to wipe her teary eyes. Romelus immediately saw the deformation of her face in shades of purple and black, but she quickly covered it again.

He grabbed her hands away from her face and asked her, suppressing the anger that devoured him, "How did this happen!?" He looked into her glassy blue eyes and then quickly pulled her to him, holding her against his chest. His jaws clamped hard as though he intended to crumble his teeth. She cried and cried and perfused over his garment before she finally withdrew from him and looked away. Again he asked—a softer voice than before as he brushed her hair from her face, "How did this happen?" He tried hard to control his trembling hand, but it was to no avail. He ripped a piece of his garment, dipped it in the nearby pond, and then gently applied the soothing cloth to her damp face as she looked into his caring eyes under the rising moonlight and the flame from a nearby torch that Romelus lit before applying the soothing cloth to her face. A cool breeze blew, rustling the multitude of different colored roses and across her face, soothing it as he wiped her tears away. After he finished refreshing her face, he sat beside her and waited for her to speak.

She was quiet for a few minutes, but he was patient. "It began not too long after we were married. At first, it was not serious; a push here and a strap there… but… always when he was drunk." His frown grew deeper and his fist clenched tighter. "Sometimes I come to the tree with a bruised back and side from him slamming me against the wall and kicking me when I am on the ground." She broke into tears and Romelus pulled her to him once again without saying a word, his dark eyes cold with fury. "L…ast n…n…ight was the worst," choking on her words with deep sorrow, "He was uncontrr… rollably drunk, b…b…but wanted to lay with me." He gave her a gentle squeeze, which seemed to calm her down a little. "He got upset when he could not perform and started beating me. He said I should be more appre…(sob) ciative of his manhood. He slammed me into th… the… side of the bed, and then laid h…h…his fist against my… face (sob). The flash of light distracted me from the sudden pain that ached my cheek, b… ut although I was d… azed, I saw the backside of his h…h…and come down across my mm…outh. I tasted blood from my l…l…lips as I fell on the floor beside the bed___ H… he ki…kicked me to… unconsciousness (sob)." She fell silent against Romelus with his blood rushing hotly through his veins as he held her tightly to him letting her cry some more. She trembled in his arms as he rocked her, trying to calm her.

He knew it was not the time to speak and waited for a few minutes before saying, "There is something that I wanted to tell you from the first day we met." She turned and looked up into his eyes. He still held her in his arms even though she was calmer. "I was in love with you from that day, and though I knew that we could never be, for I am a slave and you are my mistress, it was being with you that took me out of the reality that I am in bondage." The words seemed to melt her: softening her beautiful eyes. "I said that in the hopes that out of the simplicity of my love, you could have some peace knowing that at least one man in this world cares for you and loves you very much." He fell silent as she gazed passionately into his face. He could feel her glassy eyes on him but did not look down.

She set herself upright and away from him; she reached out and turned his gaze towards her, responding pleasantly, "I have known that for some time, poet, and true, we could never be, but your loving kindness is what kept me strong. It was your kind words in poetry that made me look forward to the next day that we could sit and read together. Do you have one today? For I could surely use one." He pulled from his parchment a poem, which she took from him saying, "I will read this one today, and do not help me." She opened the parchment, leaned into the nearby light, and started reading clumsily. He smiled.

Slavery's sorrow has always been on me
From the day I was born till presently
And though life was hard, it changed for the best
When you entered it, I must confess

I know fate is such that we cannot be
For you are married till death sets you free
So I'll stand my ground and serve your needs
For the rewards will come from my good deeds

You've mentioned about a living God somewhere
If He could hear me, He'll answer my prayer
And grant me freedom from this bondage I'm in
And give me a chance, for your heart I must win.

"___This is a beautiful poem Romelus, but you should know you already have my heart," she whispered as she wiped the tears from her face, revealed her usually breath-taking smile, and leaned against him. "I know, Nikkia___ but I can only share my love to you through my poetry." They sat silently for a while in each other's arms before parting company for the night.

Eight

Romelus thought about Nikkia and about the living God she mentioned many months ago before finally dozing off to the sound of crickets chirping in the night. He awoke the next morning and went out into the field to help Kimbi and another slave called Ato. The cool morning air blew through the fields as they worked. He worked silently as the day progressed. Kimbi turned to Romelus stating inquisitively, "A denarius for your thoughts."

Ato slapped Romelus on the back in a rigid but friendly way, sprawling him on the ground and adding, "We know you are accustomed to working on books___ it is good to see you helping us today… but it would seem that you want to leave our company." They laughed at the stale joke before Romelus stood to his feet.

"Have you ever heard of a living god? Nikkia mentioned some months ago… that he was the god of the Jews."

"Nikkia, is it?" Ato insinuated. He playfully slapped his friend across his head while he looked over to Kimbi mischievously. "Isn't that master's beautiful wife?" They laughed at Romelus as they continued to work, implying there was more to him and Nikkia. Little did they know how close their insinuation came to the truth.

After a brief silence, Kimbi turned to Romelus and replied earnestly, "I have not heard of a living god, but anything is possible."

"Well___ if there is a living god, he has to be better than the gods the Romans serve," Ato added.

They continued working while Romelus soaked in their words. After a few minutes, he said to them, "You are right___ Jupiter and Janus have not done a thing for me, so this god of the Jews might." They did not say anything more as they continued working under the sweltering sun. Romelus ended before his two friends. He made his way to his quarters to do some more work on the books for the library, and after, he prepared for his meeting with Nikkia.

That evening, Romelus met with Nikkia at the tree, and though her body ached, she was ready to learn the Latin that he taught. He complimented her on her improved understanding of Latin: in her ability to read and to write it a little. "Thank-you, poet, for I could not have done it without you," she returned the thanks.

The sun started to set over the horizon as they conversed—birds returned for the evening, chirping sweetly in the branches above their heads when he asked, "Nikkia, can you tell me what you know of the living god you mentioned some time ago?"

She looked over to him with a smile on her face, which seemed to be healing from her bruises. She was not sure what he was talking about, so he reminded her of the crucifixion story of his pass. She then looked out onto the meadow below and started:

"Some time ago, a Jew traveling through my village stopped at my father's dwelling to see if they could trade. The trader's son, Ben-yahoshua, accompanied him… and it was he who told me about their god. He was thirteen and two years older than I was. I do not remember all of what he said___ because that was five years ago… but I remember him saying that his people had suffered many tribulations through time and was only able to overcome the tyranny of dominant peoples through the power and mercy of the living god." He followed her gaze over the meadow. "They called this god, Jehovah, who dwells on a place called Mount Sinai. From what he said, only the High Priests can go there to offer sacrifices for the sins of the people..." Romelus listened to the story of Ben-yahoshua until the stars decorated the dark blanket of the night before parting.

The sounds of grunts and moans rose from Titus's chamber later that night. His sweaty body clung to Nikkia's as he lay with her. Her face was healing but was still badly bruised from the severe beating she took a few days before. She laid uncomfortably under him, for her body was still healing as well, but she tried not to show the discomfort. After planting his seed, he rolled off her, pulling her to him. They laid there in silence before he spoke. "I have taken notice that your Latin and Greek have improved."

"The poet has been patient in teaching me." She removed herself to freshen up at a nearby basin while Titus's eyes followed her.

"Yes___ you and the slave have gotten quite close."

"To uphold the oath between my father and you, I have not and will not betray you, Titus. I am faithful to our marriage and will continue to do so despite the poet's kindness," she replied without looking at him. His tone was questioning and she knew she had to appease him. She hoped her response was effective. He lay still for a while looking at her before leaving the room. "Romelus will always have my heart and my love, while you, Titus have only my body through the bondage of marriage, which can be broken, easily… if I did not care for the welfare of my father's household," she muttered, knowing that he left. Her discontent rang clear in her voice to her only audience: herself.

Nine

Time past and Nikkia gave birth to two sons and a daughter to Titus. He had many children before these three, but with the concubines in his service. Nikkia was now twenty and had grown more beautiful over the years since her marriage to Titus. She had endured several beatings, but Romelus's love and comforting words kept her going when they met at the tree. One day, while Romelus worked on Titus's books, Kimbi came to him with a joyous smile on his face. "Come, my friend___ I need to confide in you."

"What is it that has put such a smile on your face my good friend?" he inquired. He noticed Kimbi's unusual radiance emitting from his boyish happiness that he had not seen since they were children.

Kimbi sat before him. "It has been about two months now that I found favor in the eyes of Ticha, that new concubine acquired from Asia for Titus. I was informed yesterday that she is with child and it is mine, for Titus had not yet laid with her."

Romelus looked at his friend, overcome by sadness. "Why did you do this thing, my friend? This will surely bring death upon you."

"Because I love her beyond the boundaries that death could bring," he replied without hesitation. Romelus reflected on the love he had for Nikkia and understood what his friend meant. "After tonight's feast, I will take Ticha away from this place because the guests will be overwhelmed with wine and would prove to be the best time to leave." He patted Romelus on his shoulder. "My friend, I have known you since we were children, but tonight___ I will leave this place and make myself a free man___ and I will feed my household with the fruit of the earth."

He hugged Romelus and rose to leave when Romelus called out to him asking, "Where will you go? For Rome is wide spread."

"We will go to Ticha's home-land___ a place called China." He turned and left.

That night, Kimbi performed while Ticha waited for him near the gate. She pretended to be sick so she would be excused from the feast. She was a beautiful woman with long straight black hair. Her brown eyes were pleasing to look into and her tanned skin only enhanced her slender body. She waited with three of Titus's horses: one of them laden with gold and silver stolen from Titus earlier that night. Ato provided the horses from the stable and it was he who prepared them for the journey. Two days of water and provisions were distributed between the two horses ridden by the couple, and the third horse was laden with the gold and silver. When Kimbi finished his performance—he left—Romelus immediately took his place. He recited for a long time while Titus and his guests indulged in stronger than usual wine served by slaves who knew of Kimbi's journey.

Many days passed before Titus missed Ticha and inquired about her to find that Kimbi was missing as well. He immediately spread the news of his missing slaves by way of pigeons to people of power who sent word to those who traveled the roads and to the Generals who knew Titus. He questioned all his slaves who lied about not knowing of Kimbi's escape. In the end, Ato was penalized because he was held accountable for the horses in the stable, and three were missing. Titus had him tied to a stake—witnessed by his entire household, while a Roman working in Titus's service stood behind him with a short staff lined with nine leather straps and riddled with bronze spikes. When Ato was secured, he commenced flogging him, tearing chunks of flesh from his body. Blood sprayed from Ato's back as he shrieked out in pain. The sound of the strap slapping across his body echoed across the yard and pounded heavily on the hearts of the gathered slaves. Ato's cries grew fainter and fainter before he died on his knees and tied to a stake. He was removed and buried as Titus turned without a word and walked away, for his message was sent to his household that he was master and should not be defied.

The days turned to weeks then to months, but Kimbi and Ticha never re-surfaced. Kimbi was smart enough to stay off the Roman roads and avoid large Roman cities along his journey. He traded with Gaelic people, trading his horses for camels and the stolen gold for water and provisions. The time came when Ticha gave birth to Kimbi's first son and he called him Katos. They journeyed on for two years, living off the spoils they took from Titus, but they managed to earn additional possessions from the use of the gold and silver they stole. Soon, his wealth was immense, and he found himself traveling in a company of merchants on their way to Egypt. The shackles of slavery seemed lifted from him on his journey, and he soon forgot about his troubles. He was blessed with another son when he reached Egypt, naming him Lucos. They stayed in Egypt for one year before setting out for Damascus on their way to China by way of India.

Three years had passed since their flight from Rome, and Katos was two years old with his brother only a few days old. Kimbi and Ticha loaded up their belongings and started on their journey, but fate was such that on the road to Damascus, they came across a legion. The traveling legionaries, being isolated from civilization, fell upon Kimbi, slaying him and his son Katos, but Lucos managed to escape death through the hands of a stranger traveling with them who managed to escape: he took Lucos to China in a different time where he left Lucos in the care of Monks at a temple there. The legionaries, starting with the Generals down the line of command to the common legionaries, took Ticha. Her cries of pain and suffering grew fainter, along with her struggle, as she wept to her death after almost three days of none-stop violation as they passed her from one man to another. She died under a legionnaire: finally finding peace.

Ten

Romelus was now twenty-three years old and was working on translating literature for Titus. He removed himself from his work for a walk in the garden, and then he made his way to the gladiator's training ground. He saw Nikkia in the distance playing with her children, whom he was charged with teaching during the early after-noon, but he still met with Nikkia in the evenings at the tree. His body had grown stronger, much like Kimbi's, but he was not clumsy as his friend was. Titus sat watching his gladiators train during a morning of trading in olives, wheat, and livestock for fresh lions and rare tigers from Asia. The animals were secured to chains while Titus walked before them choosing the choicest ones. He taunted them to see which would react ferociously and made his decision that way. Romelus stood on a platform above looking down at the scene before him as Titus chose from the animals. After making his selection, he turned away from the creatures and made his way to the bargaining table where the merchants awaited to settle on a price with him on the goods he selected. At that instant, one of the beasts broke its chain and leapt forward towards Titus. Romelus jumped off the platform onto the tiger as it sprang at Titus, who turned at the sound of the tiger's roar so close to him to see Romelus landing on the beast that almost took his life. Romelus choked the beast as he wrapped his arms around its neck; his legs followed suit around the tiger's stomach. The beast thrashed around the earth, clawing at Romelus's hands and crushing him under its huge body.

The attendants placed a loop around the tiger's neck attached to a long pole and commanded Romelus to roll off the beast. He did so, and as his body hit the dirt, they jerked the beast back and caged it. The traders apologized to Titus for the incident and made a gift of the beast to him. Nikkia heard the commotion and made her way hurriedly to the scene to see Romelus wrestling with the beast before the merchant's men brought it under control. She wanted to go to him after the incident but saw Titus and went to him instead as he made his way from the trading.

She caught up with him. "The poet has shown great bravery in saving your life; wouldn't it be fitting that the reward of his freedom be granted to him for his deed?"

"He has shown his worth by giving me life when he sacrificed his own, but I need him for the work he does___ and you are fond of him as well."

She fell silent as they walked___ then added, "The other slaves and your guests have seen his bravery; to hold him captive much longer would cause unrest among your slaves, and Caesar would not be pleased to know that you have not rewarded Romelus once the traders meet with him." They stopped at the entrance of the coliseum. Titus thought about the idea for a while then called a nearby slave and ordered him to bring his household into the coliseum, as well as the merchants who witnessed Romelus's deed. The slave obeyed and ran off to spread the word.

"It would be favorable upon you to give the slave, along with his freedom, a horse, live stock, and two camels, for he has been a slave all his life and has nothing to start his new life with."

Titus, still a little shaken by the event, walked off saying, "He will get all that you say and some gold and silver with provisions and water for his journey." He disappeared into the coliseum while Nikkia turned on her heels and ordered a slave to fetch her children and bring them to their father in the coliseum.

Romelus sat motionlessly on the floor where he fell—thinking of his near death—once again with a wild beast. He rethought his actions as foolish for endangering his life for someone who held him in bondage. Nikkia came to him with a smile on her face. "Poet… take heart___ you have earned your freedom. Come quickly to the coliseum, for Titus is waiting with his household to grant this that is yours." She helped him up and guided him to the coliseum door where they entered, and then she left him and made her way to Titus's side with a broad smile on her face.

Titus sat elevated above his people while they sat waiting behind Romelus who stood in the center of the coliseum before Titus as the slaves sat behind on the coliseum floor. After a moment of silence, Titus opened his mouth and said in a loud voice, "This slave as of this moment___ is now free, for he has delivered my life from the jaws of the tiger." Cheers filled the coliseum. "He will part from my household a free man with animals and gold and silver and provisions and water to start his life. The gladiator who slays this tiger in battle will win his freedom as well." He turned and summoned the traders to follow him, leaving Romelus with a smiling face as the slaves cheered for him before returning to their work.

Eleven

Romelus left with some slaves for a bath where they placed a toga over his body as a sign of his freedom and Roman heritage. The horses and camels, and all that was promised to him, he received under Nikkia's care. He made his way to his quarters for the last time and looked around; then he walked around the garden into the evening. Titus had left for a journey to a neighbor's to trade with him, and his children accompanied him for the ride so they could learn the art of negotiations from him. He looked out to the tree and saw Nikkia sitting there. His heart felt heavy as he watched her from the garden and remembered the first time he saw her there all those many years ago. She was more beautiful to him now than she was then.

Nikkia sat under the tree with tears in her eyes as he sneaked up behind her. She jumped when he greeted her, and for the last time, he gazed at her as he dried her tears away before silently embracing her saying, "Thank-you, Nikkia, for being so kind to me and for convincing Titus to grant my freedom." He knew Titus well enough to know that he would not have let him go if she did not have something to do with convincing him otherwise.

Her tears continued to pour on his new clothes as she replied, "And t…thank y…you, poet, for sh…sharing my love and for comf…forting me when things go badly___ (sniff)___ m…my heart will always b…be with you___ because I l…love you___ (sniff)." She composed herself a little. "I will have no one to talk to once you are g…one, but you have earned your freedom and it w…would have been wrong to deny you that for my comforts."

He held her in his arms as he cried on her shoulders. He could hear her teeth chattering under the uncontrollable spasms of her jaw muscles. He released her saying, "I have a poem for you my dear; I hope you like it. Do not read it until I leave, for I might be tempted to stay in bondage." He handed her a parchment and looked into her brilliant blue eyes that shone under the evening moon, and he said under the sparkling stars, "I could not leave without saying good bye to you, my love, so here I am." He gazed into her eyes as the leaves from the tree blew off under the power of the wind. His long hair lifted off his face as her blue eyes locked into his brown orbs. His heart raced in his chest sending warmth through his body. "Forgive me for what I am about to do, for if I were to die tonight, I will die happy knowing that I shared a kiss with you." He leaned down to her inviting lips as she received him with flushed cheeks. Their lips locked for a long time as their bittersweet tears mingled; their hearts soared from the long anticipated kiss that swelled and grew over years of suppressed love. The cool breeze intensified, blowing their clothes and hair as it shook the tree of its blossoms that floated around them. They parted from the kiss as slowly as possible, gazing into each other's eyes; he rounded his hands away from her waist as she reluctantly released the back of his neck, running her fingers through his hair. They parted that night for the last time when Romelus walked away without looking back. Nikkia watched him ride into the night from where she stood.

Tears rolled down her cheeks and her lungs heaved in the fresh air. Romelus stopped some ways off and looked back to the tree where Nikkia stood and said to himself while drying his tears, "I pray the god of the Jews will give me a wife like you, Nikkia. You will always be in my heart." He turned, with the memory of her silhouette branded on his soul, and rode off on his journey to find this Mount Sinai so he can find the living God.

Nikkia walked around the tree that night while a full moon shone brightly in the sky. She missed him and did not know if she would ever see her poet again. She opened the poem and started to read:

Oh Goddess of Love

Oh goddess of love
You have shown me peace
You have comforted me
And loved me secretly

I loved you through my poetry
And our meeting on this hill
A slave in love with his Mistress
A Mistress in love with her slave

I am a free man now
So may I be granted one chance

To see you again that I may see
Where all my hopes and dreams began

Goodbye my love; till we meet again
Wherever I go, know that I love you
And peace will always be with you
No matter what pain you bear

We will look at the moon together
No matter where we are
And may the God of the Jews
Grant our love in another time

She folded the paper, tucked it away, and then dried her tears. She looked towards the moon and smiled, and then she turned and made her way back to her home.

Twelve

Romelus made his way south of Rome to the Mediterranean Sea and bought the service of a vessel on its way to Egypt. The vessel made stops at Crete and Malta where trading commenced for several months before setting off to Egypt. He sold one of his camels and bought a ram and three goats. His skill in trading, which he learned from Titus over the years, enabled him the double his assets on the island of Crete, but before sailing from Crete to Malta, he converted much of his holdings to gold and silver for ease of transportation. Many of his traveling companions were legionaries and other traders in silks and spices from Asia who were on their way back with the spoils of their trading. When Romelus sailed from Crete, he had with him, aside from the gold, his horse, a camel, a ram, three pregnant goats, and provisions to last the journey to Egypt.

On their journey to Malta, a storm brewed over the sea, causing deaths and loss of goods. Fortunately for Romelus, none of his possessions were lost. He managed to secure his holdings below deck during the storm, keeping them safe. The waves lurched violently against the vessel, tossing it around like a twig in a raging flood. People fell over-board while mothers tried to protect their children. Romelus returned above deck to assist the crew in securing the vessel after delivering his belongings below. A Centurion commanded his men to get the women and children below deck while the sailors ran around working on tying the ropes that secured the sails to the main mast. They also tried to get as many provisions below deck, and though they managed to save some of the goods, much were washed over-board under the puissant waves. Lightning filled the sky, piercing the cumulus nimbus clouds that hovered over the sea as it connected with the fierce ocean around the ship. The children's cries became smothered under the heavy roll of thunder that followed closely behind the lightning as boards from the vessel broke off and scattered in the water. Finally, the storm blew away as suddenly as it came, leaving behind the destructive loss that many aboard the vessel experienced.

The merchants who survived came to Romelus to buy some of the provisions he had till they reached the isle of Malta, which he sold to them. However, there were those who lost everything and were distressed at the loss came to ask favors of some food while the soldiers tended to the dead and mended what they could. They did not attack him, for they feared him since he still wore the clothing which Titus provided, making him look like an important person traveling from Rome to Egypt. He divided his provisions equally among those who lost everything after setting aside his best for the Generals on board as well as the captain of the vessel. His generosity won additional favor for him, and he was left alone on their voyage to Malta. When they neared Malta, he saw the sorrow in the eyes of the merchants who lost everything during the storm and went to them. He had the silver and gold that he received from the other merchants for the provisions of food he sold to them, so he divided the precious metals among those without anything so they could trade at Malta. They thanked him for his kindness when they came to port for repairs on the vessel. The task took close to a year, so Romelus stayed at Malta trading. While he camped at the Generals of Rome's tents and ate their food, his goats gave birth, which helped his wealth increased two folds from his trading.

When the vessel was repaired, they climbed on board and started for Egypt. Romelus brought on board two camels, two rams, eight female goats with five kids, gold and silver, which were protected under the legion who found favor in him after the storm, and new clothes and sandals for his travel. He hired the help of a servant who wanted to go to Egypt and agreed to carry the provisions aboard and to help him on the journey as payment for passage.

The merchants who lost everything during the storm came to him, for they were able to make double from what they lost and paid him twice what he gave them. He refused but receded when they would not take no for an answer.

"Where are you heading?" one of them asked him, but he lied, because he knew the Romans did not like the Jews very much, for they failed to worship their gods.

"I'm on my way to trade in the East."

The journey went without event and they finally arrived in Egypt. The Generals invited Romelus to feast with them in Cleopatra's company, and he accepted, for he had heard how she captured Caesar's heart and wanted to see what charms she used. Soldiers took his holdings to the palace, and his servant took his leave with some money and two kids that Romelus brought aboard as a gift for his service. The man thanked him for his kindness and set out on his own way.

That evening, as he sat among the Generals and guests of the Queen, she appeared surrounded by her slaves, and for the first time, Romelus beheld the young Queen of Egypt and thought to himself, "*She is not as beautiful as I thought she would be. To think Caesar had a child with this woman.*"

They ate and made merriment while Cleopatra spoke to her guests in the various languages they spoke. Romelus was impressed and realized that her beauty lay in the sound of her voice and ability to communicate with others.

That night, Romelus stood looking at the moon, as he did every night since leaving Rome, hoping Nikkia was doing the same. He reminisced about his departure from her embrace, still seeing her tears when he left as the scent of her perfume tantalized him. "I love you Nikkia; from far away, I still love you." A tear fell from his left eye as he turned his back to the glow of the moonlight and turned in for the night.

Thirteen

The next day Romelus made his way out of Egypt with a caravan on their way to Jerusalem, a journey that took several months. When they reached Israel, he had been a free man for three years and had grown wealthy. He mingled among the common people and lay with their daughters, whom he found very beautiful, but he did not bare any children. He searched for the living God among them but could not find Him, so he left and made his way to the temples, spending much of his time learning about the sacrificial offerings, and then the time came when he felt ready to make his journey to Mount Sinai. He packed up his belongings and made his way towards the Red Sea; he stopped only to sleep. He had with him two servants he hired for the journey; they warned him that only the High Priests ventured on Mount Sinai, and they had not done so for centuries. They finally reached the foot of the mountain, after braving sand storms and bandits along the way, but they did not lose anything. That night, they set up tent, and the two young men came to Romelus. One said, "It is not a good thing for a gentile to ascend to the house of God." The other agreed.

"I have heard of the marvels and the glory of your god, and from that, I cannot believe that your god will destroy me because I am a gentile. I was created by him; therefore, I am as much his child as you are." They saw they could not convince him and departed for the night.

The next day, Romelus built an altar and offered guilt offerings, burnt offerings, grain offerings, and sin offerings to God from the best of his holdings; he also offered wave offerings to cleanse himself as a symbolic gesture, stepping out of his old life into his new one.

"Take all that I have and divide it between yourselves and leave me; I believe in your god from the teachings I have heard, and soon he will be my god as well, and He will provide me with everything I need." The young men divided his holdings between themselves and left him there at the foot of Mount Sinai.

Romelus looked at the mountain and called out many hours after the young men left him, "Lord, god of Abraham, god of Isaac, god of Jacob, I have heard of you from a far land and have come here to make you my god. I have made burnt offerings like the olden days which your people have turned away from___ and now I am ready to ascend this mountain a new man and a servant before you!" He stepped onto the mountain and started climbing, but he felt heat burning his feet and quickly removed himself—knowing that the Lord was there.

An angel came to the Lord. "Most High God, a gentile is at the foot of Mount Sinai, for he thinks it is the holy mount where you gave Moses the ten laws___ Should I turn him away?"

"No, I have guided his life, and now he has given up everything to serve me. His faith in what he does not know is his strength, and the kindness he showed to those he met in distress is the wage he paid for his life."

The angel turned to walk away when God called out to him saying, "Let us test his faith in me. Go down and tell him to climb the mountain, and I will descend to him when he reaches the apex."

The angel left and went down to Romelus, appearing to him in a cloud. "Ascend the mountain to the Most High."

Romelus looked into the cloud without fear and replied, "The mountain burns my feet; how could I reach the top?"

"Romelus, ascend the mountain to the Most High." The angel disappeared, leaving Romelus alone.

He made his way to the foot of the mountain and started climbing. His sandals burnt off his feet, causing pain to rush though his body, but he did not stop. He fell many times against the steep hills of the mountain, burning his hands as well, but he did not stop. Upward he went as the flesh ripped from the soles of his feet, exposing the bones as it fried against the holy earth, but he did not stop. He was almost to the top now, but could not walk. He started to crawl the remainder of the way, burning the flesh off his hands and cartilage of his knees. He finally made it to the top where he cried out in pain, "Lord, God of Abraham, God of Isaac, God of Jacob, I am here as you commanded in pain and blood."

The Lord called from Heaven, "Remove your garments, for they stench of sinners." He removed his garments and the remainder of the sandals that wrapped his leg, and then knelt as naked as he was born on the mountain. The old garments became enflamed as they hit the earth before the Lord came down from Heaven and settled at the mountain, shaking it. Romelus looked at the cloud without flinching and was happy to be in the presence of the Most High when the Lord spoke from the cloud: "You were a slave in Rome, and I was with you. It was I who brought you out of Rome and guided you to me, for you were chosen to be the father of Love. You have offered your offerings unto me with the best of your holdings, including the burnt flesh from your own body. Your faith is strong based in the love you have for others in misery." Romelus bowed his head before the presence of God, listening as his pain lifted and his body became whole through the power of God. The Lord spoke again from the cloud and said, "Stand to your feet; I will make a covenant with you that you will be the father of Love and you will serve me, through time, doing my bidding without question for the sins that you have committed with the women of my chosen people___ who through them___ the world will be saved."

Romelus's body started transforming from his human form, growing six pairs of wings—four pairs on his back and two pairs on his ankles—lifting him off the mountain. His body became encased in an unknown material that hugged him and glittered like the stars in the sky against the blackness of the limitless universe. His long curly hair and entire eyes turned to fine gold. A sword made from an unknown substance hung from his waist as he knelt before the Lord in suspended animation. After setting him upon the mountain once again, God stepped from the cloud in partial glory. "You will be the father of Love, but because of your sin against the daughters of my children, you will serve me as a test that Love is eternal and pure in all its forms. You are human with all the feelings that go with it, but you are above human whose boundary is to walk between Heaven and Earth___ Look around you at the host of angels who fell from my grace. You will not lay with any woman and you will serve me till Love is born." Romelus obeyed and saw through new eyes, fallen angels creating havoc on the Earth.

"My God, how am I to become the father of Love when I do not have any children?"

God stood before him as Romelus knelt in his presence and replied lovingly, "You have a son." The words shocked him. "Born to a Roman widow who you took under the coliseum at your old master's feast; because of you, his off-spring will flourish and Love will come from him."

"If I cannot have a wife now, would I be able to have one once Love is born?"

"You must prove yourself to me, and in another life-time, you will find love that is yours to have. Until then, you will not touch a woman on the face of the Earth," He said while laying His hand on Romelus's head. He gave Romelus a golden ring of unique design commanding, "Take this ring and go to China to a place and time I will show to you; there you will find a young boy name Lucos at the temple. This ring belonged to his mother, Kimbi's wife, who was your friend." Romelus's heart saddened at God's words. He now knew his friend was dead, and he would never see him again. "Give this ring to him, for the next time you see this ring, it will be on the woman I have chosen for you. You must win her to you and convince her of your love, and when she accepts, the curse of loneliness will be lifted from you." He was glad for the chance of finding love: even if he had to wait forever. "While at the temple, you will learn a pugilistic art from the Monk." God revealed many things to Romelus then ascended to Heaven, leaving him to his new self.

Fourteen

Romelus tested his wings and saw that he could fly, but he was awkward at it and kept crashing against the mountain. After several hours of practice, he learned to land and maneuver through the air, but he still needed to work at it. Because he did not want to delay God's command, he flew high over the mountain and then made his way to China to the place and time the Lord revealed to him. He killed a cow there and made clothes with the hide to cover the glory of God that embraced him. His wings receded into his body, but the armor that covered him and his hair remained as they were. His eyes changed to their dark-brown color as he made his way through the mountains to the temple near Chendu. He walked through the bamboo patches and admired the birds singing in the mulberry trees above, picking at the sweet fruits and dropping the seeds to the dusty earth. After making his way up the landscape, he looked out towards the horizon and saw people working the rice fields in the distance along the Yangtze River. There at the river, he saw Lucos, now six, practicing a pugilistic form, and not too far away was his teacher, the Monk, who cared for the boy. Romelus approached the Monk. "I thank my God for guiding me to you."

The Monk turned to him and replied in his tongue, "Strange, you are the second traveler who came to me speaking my tongue. The first was a stranger who brought this boy to me, and now you. He said the same thing you said as well. What can I do for you, stranger?"

"I have a gift from the Lord for Lucos there___ a ring belonging to his mother when she was alive. I was also sent to learn the pugilistic arts."

The Monk saw the peace in his eyes and knew he was sent by a higher power, so he agreed to teach him. He saw that Romelus learned at a pace far superior to any of his pupils and had mastered the *Five Beasts Eight Method Form* within a year. He marveled at his inexplicable strength and independence from food for sustenance. Romelus stayed in China experiencing the four seasons, seeing the blossoms of spring and falling leaves of autumn.

After he mastered the pugilistic art, he gave Lucos the ring saying, "Your mother's gift to you." He walked away leaving the boy in silence. As Lucos looked at the ring, Romelus disappeared along the riverbank where the Lord appeared to him.

"When you see that ring again, you will know your wife, and you will know that I am the Lord whose words will be kept. Now Anglicize yourself and leave this place. Go to the outskirts of Damascus; there you will find a legion from Rome who sinned against me. Go there and destroy them for what they have done." The Lord returned to the heavens leaving him behind.

Romelus said his goodbye and told Lucos how much he looked like his father, and then Romelus left, walking down the mountain. He transformed, once again, and flew to Damascus to his time and to the place the Lord showed him to go.

Fifteen

The legion slept that night not knowing what was in store for them as Romelus hesitated over the camp while he watched them. He looked into the camps of the legion and then in those of the Generals. He saw one of the Generals with a woman in his arms as they moved together in heated passion. He remembered that he could not indulge in such things till Love is born. He thought on the matter as the passion heightened then fell to silence, and they embraced each other. He rose to the sky with sorrow in his heart when an angelic figure approached him.

"What troubles you?" She was very beautiful, with silver hair and baby-blue eyes, as she floated before Romelus. Her beauty could not be compared to anyone on Earth, but in his clouded state of mind, he did not pay too much attention to her appearance.

"The Lord said I am not to touch a woman of this Earth until Love is born." His wings looked graceful under the stars that reflected shimmers of gold from his hair and from the tips of his wings.

"God will not deny his servant the pleasures of the flesh. Come with me, and I will show you women whom the lord has ready for you." She guided him to a place near Damascus to a tent of people reveling in wine and various sexual perversions. Romelus watched as the angel made her way into the crowd, indulging herself with three men, before calling to him. "I am an angel created by god___ and look how he has rewarded me___ Come___ Take as many women as you want."

Romelus descended to the scene as women came to him, but before he reached them, he cried out, "Lord, what is this temptation!?" He looked at the other angel and remembered about the fallen angels that God told him to behold. He looked around the room and saw other fallen angels not seen by the people tempting them in sin. He turned and flew into the night—leaving them. Golden tears fell from his eyes to the dusty earth below and his body swelled with desire.

The Lord appeared to Romelus as he made his way to the Roman camp. "Oh servant of mine, you have made me glad today by facing sin head on and not indulging yourself. From this day, you will know those who are fallen and those who are with me," Romelus's face still showing the burden he must bare, "but temptation will come to you stronger through time, and the love you have for your descendants is the strength that will pull you through."

The Lord left, instructing Romelus to destroy the legion then to return to Mount Sinai. Romelus made his way to the camp, and with a powerful flutter of his wings, he caused a sandstorm to cover it, immolating everyone unto God and hearing their cries as they breathed their last. Fallen angels rushed in, bound the souls of those who died, and carried them off as tears fell from his eyes on his way back to Mount Sinai.

Upon reaching Mount Sinai, Romelus called, "Lord, I did as you commanded, and I am here now." The Lord appeared.

"My covenant with you will be strengthened today so you will know that I am the Lord who keeps His word." Romelus knelt.

"I have done your bidding and the legion is dead___ though I do not know the purpose of their death. What is your bidding now, my Lord?"

"Arise, and look at what I will show you. I will show you the future of your seed who is to become Love so you can see that I am your God who will keep the covenant made between us." The Lord opened a parchment against the sky and commanded him, "Read now of your seed."

Romelus started to read what the Lord revealed to him. He learned about his descendent, Richard, who will become Love and how he will bind Lucifer some time in the future.

Part Two
Fulfilling A Covenant

He will cross the threshold of time
And face all odds to be in your arms
To experience ultimate comfort
Within your loving charms

One

"I have shown you the future of Love so you can behold my glory. I know many of the terms used would be confusing to you, but in time, you will be able to understand too," the Lord said. "Now gather yourself, for I am sending you to a place of ancient times. There, you will live among the people, but remember our covenant, for the people are evil there___ and Lucifer has taken them." Romelus listened, still overwhelmed with the new knowledge of his son. "I am the future, the present, and the past. You will now journey to the past." A dark cloud covered the mountain and Romelus found himself in the past, near Beersheba.

"Go to the city of Sodom and live among the people, but revel not in their sin. You will be tempted and the pleasures of life will haunt you, but remember our covenant." Romelus descended to Earth and disguised himself as a merchant in oils that the Lord provided. He made his way to Sodom and entered the city by night where men approached him shouting, "Come lay with us, for you are new here!"

"No, but you can guide me to a place where I can sell my goods, for I will be staying awhile."

They attacked him, but he fought them off using the pugilistic arts he mastered in a future China. They fell back under his blows and amazing strength that did not leave him in his disguise. They thought to themselves, and one of them spoke. "There is a place in the market where you can peddle your goods and sleep." He thanked them and went on his way, leaving demons hovering overhead.

"We will seduce him later when the joys of our city over-power him," they conspired among the group as Romelus disappeared in the distance under the cover of darkness. They separated and entered into reveling with each other and with women on the street.

Romelus found a place and pitched his tent. That night, he wandered around the city stopping at the different sites where people gathered. The overwhelming power of fornication filled him with desire, but he controlled himself not to indulge. Harlots pulled on his garments as he walked—feasting his eyes on the beautiful women selling their bodies—others were fighting in the dark. He even saw men and women robbing each other in gambling and theft, but it was his covenant with God that drove him to the brink of insanity, for he could not indulge in the many sensual pleasures before him. He felt himself bursting with hedonistic desires as he ran into a dark corner, removed his disguise, and then darted into the starlit night while flashes of beautiful women possessed his mind—beckoning him to return.

As he flew around, his mind raced on dealing with the hard task before him. He flew towards Heaven's gate and called onto the Lord: he did not enter because his body was not glorified.

The Lord came to him and asked, "What troubles you?"

"I cannot stay in the city, for the temptations are too great," he answered from his prostrated poise.

"You can move your tent to the borders between Sodom and

Gomorrah; now go, for someone needs your help." Romelus turned and returned to Sodom. He heard the cry of a woman coming from a dark place behind a tent and approached to see ten men violating her. One of her legs lay limp to one side while three men held her arms and her good leg down. The others lined up waiting their turn while their friend penetrated her as a hand muffled her useless scream of displeasure. Romelus became enraged, and with a mighty gust of wind from his wings, he blew the men off their feet and watched them slam into a nearby pillar, killing most of them. He swooped down, gently lifted the girl into his arms, and shot into the air as she fainted in his arms making his way to the outskirts of the city between Sodom and Gomorrah, "Everything will be fine," he whispered. He was glad to free her from her ordeal, but his covenant consumed him.

The next morning, the girl awoke in Romelus's tent. During the night, he moved from the city to the outskirts and disguised himself again.

"Good morning. What is your name?" Romelus asked when he realized she was awake. She looked down to her foot and found that she could move it. She sat up, still dirty from her dance in the mud the night before.

She looked at Romelus and replied in a tired voice, "My name is Andoma; I thought my leg was broken."

"It was broken, but it is now healed. Do you want something to eat?" He handed her some bread, meat, and a pitcher of water. "I must go tend to my flock that I purchased this morning. There is a well just outside where you can draw water to clean yourself, and there are garments in the corner you can take to cover yourself, for the ones you have now are ruined." She looked at him, a little timid, but was quite comfortable in his presence as she thanked him.

"Your tongue is strange even though I understand. Where are you from?" she asked as he walked away.

"From a land very far from here." He left. His language changed to that of the time and place under the power of God. The change was strange to him at first, but he was glad that he was able to communicate with the people of this time.

That evening, Romelus returned to his tent with the livestock the Lord provided through the sale of the oils. The fragrance of fried meat filled the air, tickling his nostrils as he made his way over to his tent. He stopped short at the corner of his tent upon seeing Andoma brooding over a fire. Her long black hair dangled neatly over the garments he left her that morning as she smiled to herself and made her way into the tent. Her youthful smile touched him as he watched her return with pottery and started filling them.

"I thought you would be gone by now," he stated, stepping into view. She turned in his direction with a smile.

"I would, but I do not have anywhere to go___ and since you saved me from something terrible, I must stay and return the favor for your kindness."

"Don't you have family you could go to?"

"They were killed."

"My deepest sympathy for your loss." He turned and entered the tent to find it cleaned and in order, and he smiled as he turned to see the Lord standing before him. He was startled at first but quickly bowed his greeting as the Lord lifted him to his feet. Then he asked, "Lord, am I able to eat the food the woman is cooking? Since I have no need for meat."

"Yes, you may eat___ It will only pass through your body."

Romelus thanked Him who reminded before leaving, "Do not forget our covenant."

He went outside and ate with Andoma, and as the sun started to set over the land, men and women from the city came down in great numbers.

"We want to lay with you and the girl. Come now." Romelus stood before the crowd with Andoma behind him.

"I am the servant of God, and I am forbidden to do such things." They attacked him and the girl, but he fought them off, defeating them, before they limped and carried each other off. Andoma watched from behind him as the crowd disappeared.

"The way you fight is like nothing I've seen. Where did you learn it?"

He replied as they watched the last of the Sodomites disappear over the hill, "I learned it in a far away country."

"And your strength and speed, how is it you are so strong and fast?"

Romelus turned, looked into her beautiful brown eyes, and replied soothingly, "That is a gift from God." They made their way to the tent.

"I would like to know your God."

Two

One year past while Romelus taught Andoma about the living God and his limitless grace. He acquired a servant from Gomorrah and also taught him the ways of the Lord, but a time came when Andoma fell in love with Romelus and came to him one night. She threw herself on him as he slept on his back, startling him. Romelus awoke and immediately pushed her off him demanding angrily, “What is this evil?” She seemed surprised at his reaction but approached him in a dance-like motion.

“Don’t you find me beautiful?” She placed her hand on his chest and felt his God-given armor that was ever present.

He felt the desire in him but answered, “You are very beautiful like a rising sun ___ and like a cool breeze in the heat of the day, and though the temptation is strong, I must not, for I made a covenant with the Lord.” He stepped away from her and ran outside manifesting himself as he disappeared into the night. He flew high into the sky at an incredible speed and crashed repeatedly into the moon, leaving craters behind. He exhausted himself and looked at the Earth as dust from the moon dispersed.

When he returned to Earth, the Lord appeared. “You have proven again tonight that your love and faith in me is strong. The girl did not act alone; Lucifer’s angels caused her to sin against me. Tomorrow she must offer a sacrifice to me for the sin she committed,” Romelus kneeling before the Lord, "Come; walk with me, for there is a revelation I must share with you." He rose and walked with Him.

"The people of Sodom and Gomorrah vexed me, and I will destroy the city in two days. My chosen nation, Abraham, prayed that if I find ten righteous people, I must spare the cities."

"I have lived among the people for over a year and have only met two people who are righteous aside from myself. Would you destroy them oh Lord?"

"Go. Have the two you speak of burn offerings to me and then guide them out of the city tomorrow to Zoar where they will be safe___ because you prayed for them." Romelus knelt before the Lord who ascended to Heaven.

The next day they offered sacrifices onto the Lord for their sins, and Romelus gave Andoma to his servant saying, "This is the will of God who came to me in a dream last night. Take her and love her the same way I loved you," they, staring at each other with obedient smiles in respect to the man of God, "Now take my holdings with your wife and go to Zoar, for the Lord will destroy this land tomorrow night." He turned and wandered off into the distance leaving them.

Akim, the servant, took his wife who accepted him, and they lay together that day. On the next day, Romelus returned to find them still there and was enraged. He found them giving offerings to the Lord, so he waited until they finished. He then asked, "Why are you still here?" The thunderous sound of his voice shook them. "I told you to go to Zoar___

Now go, for the Lord will be destroying this place tonight with everything and everyone in it." They hesitated, so Romelus manifested himself in all his glory saying as they knelt before him, "You have been raised by me for the past year and I have turned you away from evil. Now go to Zoar where you will be safe!"

He returned to the ground, still in his semi-divine form, and commanded the demons that clouded Andoma and Akim's reasoning to leave. "I command you to leave my people so they can depart from this place in the name of the Most High God." The demons released them, and Andoma remembered how he saved her over a year ago and asked forgiveness for trying to seduce him. He hugged them both and watched as they gathered their belongings before guiding them to Zoar so they would be safe from people coming out of Zoar to indulge in the sin of Sodom. He blinded his young couple from the sight of the revelers, and their journey to Zoar was a success. There, he bade them good-bye and returned to the sky as the sun started setting over the horizon.

The night came and the two angels who the Lord sent to destroy Sodom and Gomorrah called fire and brimstone from Heaven, consuming the two cities with all its revelers and animals as the Earth shook under the cities, bringing them to their knees. Romelus watched and heard their cries, even the cries of the innocent, as they troubled him to tears before it was all over. He looked at the full moon above and thought about Nikkia—wondering if she was looking at the moon in her time too.

"I miss you." He imagined and image of her smiling face against the surface of the moon as a source of comfort to his separation from her. He smiled as her image seemed to smile back at him.

Three

The Lord appeared to Romelus that night. "Come with me and I will reveal all that unfolded before you since you gave yourself to me." Romelus silently descended and walked with the Lord around the burning city waiting to hear what He had to say. "When you came to me, I allowed you to come near___ and gave you great powers to do my bidding." He listened as the comforting wind blew constantly through his golden hair and the metallic feathers of his many folded wings. "The temptation you have now is the curse for your sins against the women of my people, who too are paying for their sin against you." There was a pause as they walked. He noticed the unusual comfort of the wind and the presence of singing birds around that night, which was strange, and he thought this unusual behavior from the birds and wind must have something to do with God's presence. "The legion you destroyed was the legion that killed your friend Kimbi___ and took his wife till she died, but my angel saved Lucos by my hands and delivered him to the Monk who taught you to fight in a different time." Romelus smiled at the knowledge that he had a hand in avenging his friend's death. "The legion sinned against me and almost destroyed my covenant with you when they killed Kimbi's first born. The two you just saved from the destruction of Sodom are the ancestors of Kimbi, so now you know that I am the Lord and my covenant with you still stands." Romelus reflected briefly on what was just said, but he was distracted by the brilliant moon when his thoughts drifted back to

Nikkia. "You have shown great compassion for the people you encountered, and I am proud of you. Now you are to go to Egypt to a time I will give you. There you will do my bidding as I bring my people out of Egypt." Romelus understood, now, all that he did and cast away his saddened heart for the lives he took and for the ones he watched get destroyed in Sodom and Gomorrah. A cloud covered him, and once again he traveled through time. When the cloud cleared, he found himself on Mount Sinai.

Egypt stood before Romelus, a different place from what he knew when he first came in search of the Lord. He watched from the mountain for many days while the Lord revealed his wonders in the form of different plagues on the land of the Egyptians. The time came when the Lord appeared to him commanding, "My people will be freed tomorrow. You will go through Egypt tonight and destroy the first born of every household, except for those homes marked with blood. Romelus waited until midnight, and with a mighty rush, he flew over the city slaying the first born of every thing, both human and beast, leaving the sound of sorrow behind him as blood covered his sword. He was given the name *Destroyer*, for he came down and destroyed the people of Egypt.

The next day the people of Egypt rushed the Israelites out of Goshem with gold, silver, and animals while Romelus watched from afar as they made their way towards the Sea of Reeds. The Lord appeared to him and commanded, "Come and fly before my people in the cover of a cloud." Romelus did so and could hear the people praising God, and then he saw the army approaching and moved to the back of the Israelites. He covered the sky over the Egyptians in darkness while keeping light over God's people. He heard them complaining to Moses that he brought them out of Egypt to die in the desert. Then he saw God part the Sea of Reeds for his people to walk through on dry land before falling back on the army, killing everyone.

He followed in silence and saw their joy turned again to complaining about the thirst they felt. He saw God make the water sweet and fed them angel's food. Then the day came when they fought an army and won as Moses sat on a hill. After the victory, they settled at the foot of Mount Sinai as Moses went up the mountain to speak to God. He stayed there for forty days when Romelus saw the people reveling in the same evil that caused Sodom and Gomorrah to be destroyed. They made a golden calf and started to worship it while others turned to fornication, incest, bestiality, and adultery. The sight enraged Romelus, so he left with his head down when the Lord came to him and asked, "What troubles you?"

"I do not understand your people. They are easily turned away from you after experiencing your power. Their devotion to you is weak; are you sure they are your chosen people?" He was disgusted at the sight, partially because he could not indulge in the pleasures he saw that tempted him and because of their lack of reverence to God.

"They are my chosen. Because they sinned against me, I removed myself from them for over four hundred years, but I heard their cries and brought them out of Egypt free men. I have to re-educate them in my ways, for through them all the people of the world will become my children. Now go to your time to see Nikkia, but remember our covenant." A cloud covered him, and once again, he found himself on Mount Sinai on the day he was first transported to Sodom.

Four

Romelus opened his wings and flew across the Mediterranean to Rome where Nikkia lived. To him, he was away for ten years, but to Nikkia, he was only away for three. He waited till the evening when he knew she would come to the tree on the hill. He looked over the place of his previous enslavement and saw that little changed since he left, and then he saw her from up above walking towards the tree with a limp and crouched over on a cane. Rage engulfed him at the sight, knowing this was Titus's doing. She reached the hill and sat down leaning against the tree, and from her breast, she took out a parchment and started to read the poem he gave her before he left. He eagerly descended to the ground behind her and said, "It is good to see you once again, even more beautiful since I left."

She lifted her head with a bright smile on her face and shouted with glee, "Romelus, is that you!?" Her extreme joy comforted him as he came around the trunk of the tree—to her left—noticing she could not see from her left eye. He stopped in his tracks as she stood on her cane. "What happened to you, poet? Your clothes is strange and your hair is gold."

He hugged her saying, "And I have wings too," and then he took off his clothes to reveal the armor and sprouted the wings as she watched. "Sit here, and I will tell you everything."

He retracted the wings and dimmed the glory from his eyes as they sat at the tree-trunk like they did when he was a slave. He told her how he found the living God and the glory bestowed upon him, including the curse he must carry for sinning against the children of Israel. He finished his adventurous tale while Nikkia, the love of his life, listened attentively. His curiosity and compassion for her empowered him to ask about the cane and her sight after he finished.

"After you left, poet, Titus grew enraged with me. He was losing property and value in his holdings. He never got over you leaving, and the tiger you saved him from. He started drinking heavily, and one night he came home triumphant from a trade. He was so drunk, but once again, he wanted to lay with me," his expression started changing upon recalling what happened the last time she wept in his arms and anticipated that a repeat took place, "But he could not and grew angry. He kicked me and injured my leg. Since then I had to use this cane. As for the eye, after losing some property in a bad trade, he came home and put his fist across my face in the bedchamber, blinding me in the left eye as you can see." A golden tear fell from his eyes as he listened. "That is why I still come here in the evening to find peace and to look at the moon." She leaned against him as she used to do; then she looked up at him and asked, "Do you still write? I missed your poems." He could feel her fingers against his armor as though she was touching his chest, but the armor hardened so that he could feel nothing. He was grateful for that, for otherwise, he would have broken his covenant with God.

Romelus looked down at her and brushed her hair from her face. He wanted to take her in his arms and fly away with her, but he knew he could not. "I have not written a poem since I left this place, but I have something far better than that; I have the gift of healing." He stood before her as she looked up at him, reached out his hand, touched her eye as his hair became radiant, and healed her so she could see. Then, he slowly ran his hand along her damaged thigh, found the ailment, and healed it before lifting her into his arms and setting her down before him on her feet so she could feel the glory of God. She threw her arms around him as tears fell on his shoulders, but they evaporated away when it touched the armor that wrapped his body under his clothing.

After she finished crying, she released him as he said, "That is a blessing from the living God of the Jews for convincing Titus to grant my freedom."

"How did you know that I convinced Titus to free you?" she asked, surprised that he knew.

"Because, my dear, only you had the desire and power to convince Titus to free me___ and God told me so."

They sat and talked for a while under the setting sun as Romelus watched her laugh as she spoke to him. The birds sang above their heads as memories mixed with present joy made everything seem oblivious to him but her.

After a while, he hesitantly stood under the glittering stars as she looked up at him. "I will be here tomorrow to see you before I return to the calling of God." Her eyes saddened at the despair of his short visit, so he held her in his arms as she reached up to kiss him. He reached down to kiss her, but moved his lips to her forehead, kissed her, then held her tightly saying:

Thank God for this day
That I embrace you the same way
As I did all those years ago
Causing my love for you to grow

I wish I could kiss you
The way you want me to
But if I do, we may never be
For all of eternity

Just let me hold you here
And a time will come: I swear
When we could share a kiss
To makeup for the kisses we have to miss

For now, your embrace will have to do
Why? Because of the love I have for you
I've looked at the moon with teary eyes
And I'll continue to do so till I die.

He recited into her ear, causing warm tears to fall from her eyes, before parting from her embrace and lifting to the sky. "Forgive me for not kissing you___ I have a covenant to keep with God." He flew away as golden tears fell from his eyes. The burden of being alone, once again, surrounded him. He dared not look back to see her teary eyes as she waved at him, with the sound of her voice singing in his ears.

"Goodbye, poet…see you tom…(sniff), tomorrow."

Five

The next day, Romelus stood waiting for Nikkia to meet him at the tree when he heard her crying out from the garden below. He dashed to where she was and saw Titus slapping her on the ground while some of his slaves watched. His eyes became golden with rage as he flew between Nikkia and Titus. He immediately lifted Titus into the air—whose eyes showed tremendous fear. Romelus's glory shone brightly and hotly as he looked into Titus's eyes with his hand wrapped around Titus's throat.

"You dog! What kind of man are you who beat the mother of his children in the company of slaves?" his passion burning to the point of exploding, "That woman has given her life to you and is devoted to the covenant of marriage she made with you___ and this is how you repay her?" he reflected on the good times he spent with her on the tree and continued with a tightened grip around Titus's neck, "I would give all my power and glory in exchange for her; here you have a good woman, and you are treating her worse than the slaves who serve you." Titus's sweat seeped from his brow. He grabbed at Romelus's death-grip with no avail to free himself. Romelus wanted to snap his neck but remembered his covenant with God and the future of his seed.

"Wh…who are you?" His fear was intense as he held on to Romelus's hands.

"I am Romelus, the slave who won his freedom because of the virtue of your wife___ Now listen carefully: From this day forward, you are to stop drinking___ and treat Nikkia as a wife with love and respect." Titus trembled in agreement. "She is protected by the Most High God, and if harm comes to her, a torment of pain will take your body for fifty years before you die. This is my covenant with you through the wrath of God." His voice was like thunder with an electrical effect that terrified Titus. Romelus placed his hand on Titus's face, burning the shape of his hand into his cheek, and then he threw him into a nearby pond.

He descended to Nikkia who remained battered and bruised on the floor, while the slaves who saw, ran to call other slaves to defend Titus. They came with weapons and attacked Romelus, who protected Nikkia. He stood to his feet and extended his wings releasing fire and lightning on his enemies, and then he returned to Nikkia as she lay unconscious on the ground while the slaves watched from afar as Titus climbed from the pond. Romelus's rage softened as he lifted her gently into his arms to revive her. He touched her face then took some water from the pond and drenched her forehead. "Romelus," she whispered in a weak voice, but loud enough for the slaves to hear. He softened and his wings disappeared and his eyes became dark brown before the slaves realized it was he and put down their weapons.

"Poet, I cannot move my arm." He then noticed that her arm hung limply at her side, so he took the damaged limb in his hand and healed it; then, he touched her face and smiled while taking the pain away and making her whole again.

He turned to the slaves and threatened, with Nikkia comfortably in his arms, "If any harm comes to her and none of you do anything to help, the Lord will send me as the destroyer to remove every sign of your existence off the face of the earth!" He turned to Titus, who saw the *Fear of God*, and ordered, after setting his beloved down, "Take your wife and remember the covenant I made with you. Now lift your hand towards her." Titus did and felt pain coursing through his body as she shuddered, so he put his hand down. "Now___ if you ignore that pain and strike her, the pain will increase one hundred times, and if you continue to strike her, it will grow one hundred times more and it will kill you after tormenting you for fifty years."

He turned to Nikkia and said with a smile as he brushed his hand against her face, "The Lord has sent me here for a purpose and that was to bless you; now go and live in peace___ for this is the last time you will see me." She smiled at him and hugged him tightly. He could feel her tears on his armor and could see the steam as it evaporated into the air. He felt the sorrow of loneliness engulfing him once again, so he loosened her grip as gently as possible and lifted himself into the night looking down at her smiling face as a stream of tears rolled down her cheeks. She was sad that he was leaving her once again but knew he had to go. The separation twisted his heart with a pain as his hair radiated, and the golden tears fell from his eyes into her outstretched hand and settled there.

"I am sorry my dear for not being a good husband to you. Romelus showed me the *Fear of God* and now all is clear."

She looked up to Romelus with tears in her eyes then at the moon and said, "Good bye, poet___ may our love meet in another time." He disappeared from sight into the starry night as slowly as possible with his heart pulling towards her. He knew he couldn't stay, so he shot to the moon where he wrote the words, *I love you my beloved Nikkia; may our love meet in another time*. Tears of gold fell on his words; his sorrow was pounding at his heart with much vigor. He turned to the Earth and remained suspended as he looked down with his tears drifting away in the vacuum of space: his silent tears—his heartbreak—his loneliness tormented him, but he composed himself and returned to Mount Sinai.

Six

Romelus stood on Mount Sinai looking at Egypt below. He recalled the life of Richard from memory and realized that the language spoken was not anything he ever heard, but he was able to understand it. The picture that was painted seemed to be something from a distant future in his mind when an angel appeared to him saying, "Thus sayeth the Lord. Go back through time to a place I will show you, and there I will meet you and give my instruction." He raised his hands and spread his wings causing the cloud to encompass Romelus, sending him through time.

Romelus found himself overlooking a city with wide walls surrounding it. Chariots were racing on top the walls when the Lord appeared to him as he looked down on the city.

"Romelus, this is Jericho___ It is on the land I promised my people. Look before you and see how they have grown since you saw them last." He looked and saw the Israelites complaining less and not rebelling against God; instead, they stood before him a well-trained army.

"Who is that man that leads them now?" seeing the new face of Joshua.

"That is Joshua, a most courageous man___ whose faith in me can compete with yours." Romelus looked at Joshua and admired his courage and fearless demeanor.

"His lack of fear and his absolute confidence surpasses that of

Moses." The Lord laughed at the observation.

"That is true, for he was Moses's pupil who has out-grown his teacher." Romelus smiled at the comment. "In seven days, I will bring down the walls of this city. You will manifest yourself as 'The Protector,' for my people have sworn to a harlot who kept them safe. Her abode must be protected when my angels bring the wall down. You will know the place when you see a scarlet cord hanging from her window. Protect her and our covenant will not be broken."

Romelus entered the city while God's army marched around it and made his way to Rahab's dwelling and entered. "No more services are offered here," came the sweet voice of Rahab, a gorgeous woman with long black hair and bright brown eyes. The dress she wore was pure seduction revealing her long legs and feminine curves that enhanced her beauty. Her dark skin was smooth and blemish-less. There is no doubt she inspired lust in the eyes of men, and with every motion, she could name her price without resistance. She turned to see Romelus who became almost spellbound by her beauty.

"I saw the scarlet cord, and I'm here to fulfill the oath made by the children of Israel." She offered him a seat and introduced him to her family already packed for their journey, as the army circled for the sixth time. "Tomorrow, when the walls come down, stay within this room. I will lift this part of the wall from the earth and set it down before the dust clears so no one will see this, but you will feel it. Tell no one of this experience for as long as you live." They swore it to him, and then turned in for the night after he left.

Romelus hovered high over the city—looking at the moon of this time. He wondered if Nikkia still came to the tree to look at the moon but did not dwell on it; instead, he looked down at the dark-skinned people of Jericho but did not try to understand why God would destroy them.

While he hovered over Rahab's dwelling in silent meditation, Jehovah appeared to him again. "When you hear my chosen people cry out, the walls will come down into the city." Romelus nodded as He departed from him.

He looked around at angels gathering and waiting to charge the wall. The hours rolled by as the army circled the city in silence while the armies on the wall looked down at them. Romelus hovered high in the sky like a bird of prey looking down on its victim. The moment came when he heard the cries from the Israelites, and the angels charged the wall, bringing it down. The force from the falling wall that bordered Rahab's dwelling tilted it as Romelus focused himself on the structure, and without moving from his position, he lifted that section of the wall with mere thought. He set her dwelling upright again from its slight lean and placed it down onto the earth before the dust cleared, reducing the tremble to a minimum. In that instant he removed himself from the destruction.

Seven

The Lord appeared to him saying, "Go back to your time and there I will meet you, for your test will soon be over. Once you get there, I'll have a reward for you, but___ it will be one of your greatest tests. Go to a place I will show to you in Egypt, and there you will find an old slave woman blinded by fire. Heal her eyes, and she will reveal my gift to you."

Romelus bowed before the Lord and made his journey through time to his time and stood on Mount Sinai looking out over Egypt. He flew to the place God showed him along the Nile River and found the old woman. She was resting by the bank, weak with age and the labors of life. He held her in his arms and said, "The Living God sent me to your aid, so fear me not." He gave her a drink of water and rested his hands over her eyes as she shivered in his arms from the cool evening. "Open your eyes and see."

She opened her eyes, looked up at Romelus, and asked, "What are you? For I have never seen a man with golden hair and golden eyes. Are you a god?"

Romelus replied while retracting his wings and taming the glory from his eyes to its dark brown luster, "My name is Romelus, son to a slave unknown who died while saving my mother and me on a journey back from Egypt to Rome." Tears filled her eyes as he spoke. "My mother was sold to slavery, and so was I. But I earned my freedom and came in search of the living God who has transformed me into the image you see before you." Her tears flowed freely as she pulled him close to her touching his face repeatedly. He allowed her to vent her emotions. "Did I say something wrong?"

She sat up from him and looked at him saying, "Did you say your name is Romelus?"

"Yes, I am. My mother gave me the name."

She looked at him and his golden hair and said as she touched his face again, "I know, for I am your mother, daughter of a Plebeian who sold me into slavery when he found out you were the son of a slave who died on the way to Rome so our lives could be spared." The words caused blood to pump through his veins at an increased velocity making his head spin. "I gave you the name and taught you Latin and Greek before I was taken away." He looked across at her with a blank expression of shock. Then, realizing she was his mother, he embraced her.

"Why are you here by this river, mother?" he asked holding her tightly.

"Romelus, I was blinded and I'm now hunted for sport, but before you go back the your God, I want you to know that your father was a Prince of Egypt whose mother was from Asia and whose father was an Egyptian Prince. Cleopatra, who won favors with the Generals in her army to overthrow her government, sold him to slavery. You have royal blood in you, son, and your father died loving you as he did me. I prayed to the gods that I see you before I die, and it seems that your God answered my prayer." He opened his mouth to say something when the Lord called to him.

He removed himself from his mother saying, “The Lord calls, I must go, but I will return soon.”

Eight

Romelus manifested his full power and ascended into the sky towards the Lord with a smile on his face as he greeted him.

"Save your rejoicing, Romelus. Look below and see your mother's master and his men are circling her." He looked down and saw the Egyptians circling his mother with their spears, and swords, and dogs.

"I must go down to her aid!" he exclaimed, venturing to leave when the Lord commanded him.

"No! Her time to leave this world is now, but your battle for her is in her next life where you must intervene." Romelus looked at the Lord in surprise but did not move. He stood his ground and watched as the men set their dogs on his mother while tears of gold flowed from his eyes. His glory burned like the sun, but the Lord blocked it from view. His heart soared like a raging storm as the dogs bit and ripped her clothes.

"Romelus!" she shouted looking to the sky in pain, as arrows and spears severed her body giving up her ghost.

"Your battle is now. Go and guide your mother's soul to Heaven where she belongs." He shot faster than light towards his mother, his speed creating a powerful turbulence that flattened the reeds along the riverbank. The aftershock uprooted trees and toppled nearby buildings, as her soul rose from her body. The men walked away leaving her on the bank of the river for vultures and crocodiles as they made their way to a feast, but Romelus's sudden appearance frightened them. The gush of wind that followed and the destruction it caused terrified them even more as they ran.

His mother rose from her body, saw Romelus, and smiled. He embraced her in his almost glorified state saying, "I am sorry for not coming to your aid in life, for the Lord told me my battle was to follow."

"I know___ I called to your God after he called you and asked for death so I can be with you." Her tone was so reassuring that Romelus's guilt left him. "It is through your faith and love, my son, that your God answered my prayer___ so He could become my God."

He lifted his mother into his arms as she smiled up at him. He guided her towards Heaven but was stopped by Lucifer's angels who demanded in one voice, "This soul belongs to us, for we still have the keys of life given to us by Adam."

Romelus's glory manifested brighter than ever, and he replied holding his mother tightly, "In the name of Jehovah___ stand aside___ for He who is Most High commanded that my mother be brought to Heaven where she belongs." They laughed at him as his mother clung to his neck; her appearance returned to her younger self.

The Lord spoke to him saying, "Remove yourself as fast as you can to Heaven's gate where my host of angels will meet you and would take your mother through the gate. Then you create havoc among the fallen who dares defy my name." Romelus heard, and without waiting to hear what the angels were saying, darted towards Heaven while they followed. He reached the gate where angels waited for him and took his mother through the gate. She watched as Romelus turned his attention to the fallen angels.

Michael came to God asking, "My Lord, should I go out and help your servant?"

"No, for through him I will show Lucifer that he could never win against me. Romelus's faith in me has grown strong. I let him watch his mother's death and it did not move him to disobey me." Michael removed himself from God's presence and stood looking through the gate.

Romelus fought these angels as they attacked from all sides. More came in to destroy him before he removed himself from his attackers and waited at a distance. He placed his sword in its sleeve, opened his wings out wide, and as the angels moved in on him, shouted, "Behold! ___The glory of God!" He closed his eyes and lifted his arms to Heaven's gate; his entire body glowed like a thousand suns as the angels crashed into him, causing an explosion. They fell from the smoke unconscious as their companions took them back to Pandemonia while the cloud cleared from around Romelus, leaving him untouched. He opened his eyes and flew over to Heaven's gate and stopped, not giving a second thought to the battle just ended.

They opened the gate and his mother came out to embrace him. Then the Lord came to them and said, "Romelus, go and bury your mother's body. You cannot enter Heaven, but you can go into Pandemonia and bring your father. He will be reunited with your mother, for he died like the son of man: giving his life to save many lives." Romelus bowed before the Lord then returned to the Nile to bury his mother's body there. He flew into Pandemonia and beheld the beauty that he read about when he learned about his son. Lucifer, who angrily paced back and forth, cursed the wind in disgust. Romelus looked at his beauty and marveled that such a creation could become evil.

"I Am sent me for my father, whom you have. Give him to me, or I will take him by force from this place." Lucifer called to his attendants who brought out Romelus's father in chains.

"This is my world, God's little errand boy. If you want this soul, you will have to come through me." His tone was harsh and defiant.

"I am coming through you, and all of God's power and glory are coming with me."

He opened his wings and extended his arms towards his father, breaking the chains, as he moved closer. He pulled his father to him as holy light surrounded them. Romelus turned to leave, and as he left, he said, "This is a message from God: your time is near, and His power is greater than yours will ever be. You are weaker than you claim to be. When God comes, he will take what power you have now, and when my son comes, he will bind you like the fowl that you are." Lucifer sent angels after him, but they fell to the side like flies, for the glory of God shone brightly through him.

Romelus was flying with is father towards Heaven when the man looked up to him and asked, "Who are you?"

He looked down at his father and replied, "I am your son, Prince of

Egypt. I was borne of a Roman woman who awaits you at Heaven's gate. I was chosen by God to glorify His name and in so doing, bring Love into this world through my son."

"Thanks to your God. He has heard me from the pits of hell and has answered my prayers. I am Arsinoë, Prince of Egypt, sold into slavery by my sister, and I am father to Romelus. Did you know I told your mother to give you that name so you will rise up and crush the Empire of Rome that enslaved us all?" He looked at his father and saw that much of himself came from him. He reached the gates of Heaven, and it opened to him. His mother embraced his father for a long time before they entered the gate.

Arsinoë turned to his son and asked, "Are you not coming, son?" His smile and kind eyes reminded Romelus of himself.

"I have not left the Earth like you have, and the Lord made a covenant with me. My time will come when I too will leave the Earth to be with you." He turned away as the gates of Heaven closed and descended to Mount Sinai under the stare of his long lost parents.

The Lord came to Romelus there. "Your faith has made you strong. On this day, I make another covenant with you that the men who killed your mother will be cursed, and their names will be removed from the face of the Earth forever. Their children will slay them then turn their swords on themselves."

"My Lord, if it pleases you, forgive those who trespassed against me so their children do not turn on them; instead, bless them, for they inspired the strength in me to once again unite my father with my mother."

"As you say, it shall be so. You are the father of Love and have shown that today towards your enemies."

Nine

Now many years had past, and Romelus kept his covenant with the Lord. The birth of Jesus was near when the Lord came to Romelus and said, "Romelus, go to Rome where you will find Nikkia." His face lit up at the sound of her name. "Her time is near and must be escorted to Heaven so our covenant will be sealed." He lifted to the heavens and made his way to Nikkia hurriedly. There, he disguised himself as a traveler and waited for her at the tree. The evening drew near when he saw her, now an old woman, being escorted to the tree. But they did not see him and proceeded to set her down.

"Return for me when the moon stands full in the night," she commanded. They bowed and left before she realized someone was there. "Who are you stranger, that you sit silently looking on?" She leaned against the tree, undisturbed by his presence. He presented a sign that he was a mute and could not speak, so they sat silently until the moon came up. "Ah… there is the moon. Over the years I have gazed at it hoping that Romelus is out there looking at it too." She fell silent with a smile on her face before speaking again. Romelus listened, bursting to reveal himself to her. "It has been some time now since my husband died, but it was the love of a slave who kept me strong. I pray to his God every day that I will see him again before I die, but the years just came and went, and the poet never came." Her words tugged at his heartstrings. "At least we still have the moon wherever he might be." He pulled her to him in silence as they looked at the moon. "He used to hold me like this___ before he showed my husband the fear of his God___ and comforted me when my body was broken." She pulled out the poem. "He wrote this to me, so I read it every night under this moon."

She started to read until she came to the end when he recited the last line with her. "Poet, is that you?" She turned to see.

He smiled, removing his disguise and saying, "It is me, and we have watched the same moon together every night through time." Her bewildered smile of happiness captured him like the first time they spoke all those years ago. "The Lord heard your prayers and sent me to escort you to Heaven's gate, for your time is near." She embraced him, but he remembered his covenant.

"You still look the same since I last saw you. You must think that I am not beautiful any more, for I have aged and you have not."

She looked away from him, but he pulled her back saying, "I have traveled through time as the servant of God and have seen many things of beauty," her eyes swelled to the brink of tears, "and whatever time I was in, I looked at the moon. Though I saw many beautiful things, you are still the most beautiful sight to me, for it is not only your outer beauty, it is your inner beauty that keeps you near my heart." She smiled as he held her closely while her tears of joy fell on him.

"I am happy to know that you still love me." He was glad to hold her in his arms and wished he could die with her so he could hold her forever in Heaven, but his curse hung over his head reminding him that such would not be his fate.

"I am the father of Love under God's covenant with me; I would be less befitting of the honor if my love did not break the boundaries of time."

Nikkia rose and said as her slaves returned for her, "May our love meet in another time." She caressed his face and walked to her slaves, a strong woman to their surprise, with a lifted spirit. He touched his face where she touched him and embraced the quickly fading warmth from her hand. He wanted to cry but was overjoyed to see her, to hold her, to love her.

Ten

Romelus stood watching her leave when the Lord called to him saying, "Go wait for Nikkia over her dwelling, for tonight she will leave her body. Guide her to Heaven's gate and protect her from Lucifer."

Romelus hovered over her dwelling well into the night waiting for Nikkia. He was determined to take her to Heaven safely and wished the fallen would oppose him. The Lord placed her into a deep sleep and spoke to her saying, "I have heard your prayers through Romelus's grace. I make a covenant with you that your love will meet Romelus's again in another time. Now leave your body, for he is waiting to escort you to Heaven and to protect you from the fallen. Do not mention my covenant with you to him, for it will shatter our covenant as well as mine with him."

Romelus waited patiently before seeing Nikkia rising towards him. He took her in his arms as Lucifer and his angels came towards them. "Her soul belongs to me you little insect," Lucifer snared as he reached for Nikkia.

Romelus turned away from him and headed to Heaven saying to her, "Those are the fallen. Their power is nothing compared to the power of God, so do not be afraid." His faith had grown to a point that Lucifer was nothing to him. Lucifer realized this and ordered his angels to return to Pandemonia. She nestled in his arms leaning her head against his chest. He squeezed her gently, comforted to hold her, and held on to every passing moment that he held her. Her youth returned and her smile invoked a passion that burned in him.

They reached Heaven's gate, and it was opened unto them. He set her down saying, "I cannot enter Heaven's gate, for I have not given up the ghost as you have." She gazed lovingly into his eyes with a great temptation to kiss him. "Here comes my mother and father. They are once again united." She looked in the direction he indicated to see them, but quickly turned her attention back to him as they held each other and gazed into each other's eyes. She reached up waiting for a kiss. His brown eyes, filled with tears, busted open as the tears flowed down his cheeks. "I have a covenant to keep with my Lord. You are safe now here in Heaven. Go now___ In time, we will meet again." He stepped away from her comforting embrace feeling the pang in his chest increased three fold as she looked at him teary eyed.

"May our love meet in another time," she said as she stepped backward through Heaven's gate. Romelus floated away gazing at his love and disappeared slowly in the distance as his tears fell against his armor.

Eleven

Romelus stood on Mount Sinai and looked out unto the growing cities. The Romans had extended their empire and had influenced many cultures. Several years past, and Jesus was under persecution. The Lord appeared to Romelus saying, “Go and watch, for the hour is near. My son is giving his life for the world___ the same way you have given your life to me. When he is crucified, darken the skies for three hours and tremble the Earth; there, you will see my miracle.” Romelus left after bowing to the Lord.

He watched the crowd below as people threw stones and dried food at a man, and he watched as they strapped him. With every blow, he saw Ato’s death bouncing off his mind, and this thought enraged him, but he did as the Lord commanded and watched. The cruelty of the Romans had grown since his time as a youth, but he watched without lifting a finger. The hours turned into days and Romelus waited, but the day finally came when they strapped him to the cross between two men. The cries of pain brought back memories of the slaves, and the woman with child who died on the cross. He mourned for them and prayed, “Lord, let those who died wrongfully be covered in your grace!”

On the third hour, Romelus lifted his hands to the sky commanding the moon to block the sun from the Earth; then he looked towards the land and shook it.

Jesus gave up the ghost, and the skies cleared. Romelus saw his friend Kimbi and his wife rising from their graves and was pleased, but they did not see him. All around, those who died unjustly rose: all the slaves who were crucified when he was a child rose. Then he saw the woman whom he released from the cross as she came to him. In her hands was her child, held closely as she said, "Thank you for releasing me, and thank you for praying to our Father that we should be saved, oh father of Love." She lifted into Heaven guided by the angels of the Lord. He saw Rahab, and Andoma and her husband; he saw everyone whom he came in contact with, except those who died doing wrong. When it all ended, he returned to Mount Sinai and sat there looking over the valleys below.

The Lord came to him. "My son, your sins have been paid in full. I made a covenant with you, and it will be kept. Come with me, and I will show you a place where you will not be tempted till our covenant is met." He followed the Lord to an uninhabited tropical island and stood atop a mountain range.

"My Lord, why do you call me your son?"

"Your Brother who died on the cross, paid the price with his death so your soul can be once again be reborn to my family. I am no longer your God; I am your Father." Romelus stepped forward to embrace his Father, who said, "Now rest, my son, for your work is finished," while they embraced, "A time will come when I will come to you and take you to another place where my covenant with you will be fulfilled." God placed him under a deep sleep, stiffened his body to form a life-like statue, and placed him high on the mountain next to a waterfall. The Lord commanded the birds and the wild animals that lived there to keep him clean and to ward off anyone who came this way, except for the child who will become Love. He turned to the Earth and commanded it to divide itself so the journey would be impossible for anyone to climb, and then He left.

Part Three
Climax To Their Love

To wait in patience for this:

A moment just with you

He will wait till the end of time

For your love so full of bliss

One

One thousand nine hundred and seventy years came and went while Romelus stood dormant in his statue form, and the world had changed much since his time. The island where God placed him was now called Trinidad, and Richard had already been born and living with his grandmother. He lived with her from infancy while his parents built a home in the nearby city of Arima. It had been nine years now as he looked up at the two hills that protected the valley where he lived and reminisced of the life he had, for the day came when he had to leave this paradise for his home with his parents in the city.

That day he packed his clothes ever so slowly not wanting to leave the only home he ever knew. It was his one true home before stepping into God's grace many years later. As he packed, he remembered the wonderful times he had during the first nine years of his life. He remembered climbing the slope of the constant, emerald-green hillside and sitting at the top over-looking the village. He enjoyed the view with the palm trees bordering the sides of the dusty roads and the multitude of wild flowers growing freely along the front of cottages and mud huts, placing splashes of red, yellow, white, violet, and orange on the canvas of his village. He remembered lying on the soft grass on one of the hills, absorbing the cool, tropical breezes that sometimes lulled him to sleep as he spent most of his time gazing at the azure blue sky eating plump, juicy mangoes and bananas from the trees that grew spontaneously throughout the countryside.

Sometimes he climbed the other hill where he would sit under coconut trees and gaze at the crystal-green ocean in the distance below. He remembered watching small boats harbored on the ivory-white shore of that spectacular beach, while larger fishing boats came in for the morning after a night's work on the gentle ocean to sell their catch to business men from the city. After selling most of their catch, they took what was left and made trips through the villages selling the remainder at bargain prices. After the morning of community business, the fishermen returned to their homes leaving the countryside in the same peaceful harmony they found when they came. He remembered climbing the many tall, slender coconut trees to pick a few of the olive-green coconuts, and then he descended to the ground with his *cutlass*. He'd take a few of the nuts, and after slicing a hole in them, he indulged himself in the sweet coconut milk with some running down his hands before dripping off his elbows. After drinking his fill, he sliced the hard shells to eat the soft, sweet jelly that clung to the interior. When he could eat and drink no more, an old almond tree was readily disposed to offer shelter from the hot sun as he sprawled under its shade and listened to the music of the massive ocean. Below, the waves broke onto the white sand adding the finishing touch to a beautiful scenic view of the sandy shore. Most of the times he fell asleep listening to the ocean while the cool, gentle breezes constantly stroked his head.

He remembered waking up in the evenings, picking up additional coconuts, and making his way down the hillside to the village where he occasionally stopped to play with his friends and familiar village dogs that came wagging their tails and jumping all over him. As the golden sun started to sink behind the hills, it would fill the sky with rays of gold and crimson colors that reflected off the houses and huts. This reflecting light seemed to force the multitude of flowers to freshen the air with mixed fragrances that tickled his nostrils, a scent that made him long for a taste—as though it was a forbidden fruit. Other smells filled the air from the stoves inside kitchens and outside fireplaces at the various homes in the village. He remembered how the smell of food motivated him to move a little faster on his way home. The aroma of curried chicken and rice, stew chicken, fried fish bought fresh from the hands of the fishermen; hot breads, and cakes from a hundred ovens—all mingled in the air to make his mouth water to a point of drooling.

When he reached home, he would always find his grandmother cooking and sometimes tried to steal a taste of the spicy food, but she always caught him and chased him from the house. This was his signal to go down to the nearby lake for his bath with the other village children. He remembered how they ran through the dusty streets naked, except for a towel over their shoulders and a bar of soap. The noise of giggles and laughter echoed off the hills that made everyone feel safe and free from troubles. Reaching the lake, they would throw their towels on the nearby rocks and jump into the clean water that started at a spring on the top of the mountain but grew into a gentle river, which in turn, became a waterfall filling the basin of the lake. All the children soaped themselves and pretended to swim while their feet walked on the lake's bed as a weak current gently pushed the overflow down the mountainside. He remembered watching the sunrays reflect off the waterfall's misty spray, creating rainbows that kissed the day goodbye and then returning quietly to the body of water that made it divine. After the fun of bathing, they dried themselves quickly and rushed back to their homes like hungry goblins ready to devour the delicacies that awaited them.

He remembered hurrying home, putting on his underwear, and dashing to the porch where his grandmother brought their dinner. They usually ate watching the sun set in the orange and red sky. The dish she served was always good with spicy, mouth-watering gravy smothering the plain rice. He dug into his plate, stuffing every inch of his mouth with her delicious cooking, like a vulture that showed no mercy, and he cast an occasional glance in his sweet grandmother's loving eyes as she watched him eat. After dinner was finished, he helped her clean the dishes and threw the trash away in a place selected where it can decompose into the earth.

After dinner, his grandmother sat with him and played cards on the porch with their source of light coming from the radiant flame of a kerosene lamp, which shared just enough light for them to see the cards. They played while watching for his grandfather and his uncles, Damian and Steven. Damian is the uncle who taught him how to read and write; Steven is the uncle who taught him to play games and climb *fatpoke* trees.

They usually arrived around the same time each day from school and from work under the bright moonlight and bejeweled sky of stars.

Seeing through a haze of tears, Richard packed his belongings and left them on the porch. His great sorrow spun his head to dizziness with the thought of leaving the only home he ever knew. His dear grandmother came to him, comforted him against her bosom, and whispered into his ears, "Son___ when yuh go to de city wit yuh muda, grow up an' make meh proud___ 'cause you is meh black gold." The comforting words of his grandmother did little to comfort him as the tears continued to flow.

After gathering himself, he took a last walk up the mountain and wandered around aimlessly. The Lord guided him, causing the earth and the dangerous animals to clear his path as he wandered to the stream where Romelus stood, not dead, but asleep. Richard beheld his ancestor in full glory, but he was scared and ran back the way he came. The earth moved, silently removing the path so no one could come that way, and the animals returned to guard Romelus. Richard raced home but did not say a word of what he saw. He waited for his mother to arrive as his friends came to say goodbye.

His mother finally arrived driving an ugly yellow pickup truck and took him away to the polluted city. The emerald-green leaves, the white foam on the sandy shore, the assorted rainbow of flowers, and the heavenly blue sky of the country was a paradise that disappeared from view as they drove away. He learned to love the city, but home to him would always be in the serenity of the tropical countryside, Trinidad's best scene to him. His parents divorced three years later, and he moved to America (as it was written) leaving his world behind to start a new one.

Two

Thirty years passed after Richard assumed his new role in the heavens, and Romelus walked upon the Earth once again. For the past thirty years, he worked diligently to fit in and eventually found himself a job translating manuscripts of ancient Greek and Latin for a prominent public library in Richmond, Virginia. Before landing this job, he spent much of his time in schools getting an education and had multiple identities over the years since he did not age. He stood at the bus stop, at the corner of Monument and Malvern Avenue, waiting for the bus under his umbrella. The dark clouds covered the spring sky, dimming the radiant glow of the sun as lightning performed its dance against the earth to the deep drum-roll of thunder that brought up the rear. The tall trees that bordered the streets looked dark and murky as rain dressed the leaves and trunks that glistened from the lightning that commanded the sky. Cars rolled by—some "flying," while others were more cautious. Across the street, children ran from a bus that stopped and made their way to a nearby high school a block away carrying their book-bags over their heads. He looked up the street in the direction his ride came and saw it in the distance through the curtain of raindrops. The bus pulled up just as the traffic light turned red, and the driver opened the door. Romelus welcomed the warm, dry interior and quickly shut his umbrella before jumping in.

"Good morning, sir."

"Good morning. Nasty weather we're having," the bus driver replied as he chuckled a little. His tired face looked beaten by a lifetime of hard work.

"Nah, it is not too bad; the rain is good for the trees," Romelus responded as he paid the toll. He walked to the back of the almost empty bus and took a seat near the exit door. His umbrella dripped before him as he wiped his hands against his baggy jeans and adjusted his T-shirt into his pants, a different look that suited him compared to the Roman toga he wore in ancient times or the armor that embraced his body in the service of the Lord.

Many people boarded and left the bus at different stops along the road as Romelus kept a watchful eye for his stop, which came about half an hour later. He quickly pressed the bell and stood waiting at the exit. The doors pulled open and he stepped out into the rain, quickly opening his umbrella. He stood on East Main Street, looked both ways, then crossed to the other side making his way down the street. After walking about a block, he heard a familiar voice calling out to him. "Seth! Seth!" A woman ran up to him wrapped in a raincoat. When Romelus took on this new life, he took on the modern name of Seth Anthony Lover.

He turned and smiled saying, "Good morning, Cindy."

She grabbed his arm and pulled the umbrella over her head. "Pick up the pace Seth, my shoes is getting wet." She locked her arm in his and pulled him along as they both shared his umbrella. After a moment of pause, she replied, "Mornin' to you Seth."

The library came into view after a few blocks, so Cindy pulled Seth a little faster up the steps to the shelter of the library's entrance where a guard opened the door and greeted, “Mornin’ y’all.”

Three

They made their way to the employee's lunchroom where Cindy took off her raincoat and hung it in a corner to drain. Seth handed her his handkerchief to dry her drenched face as she looked down at her wet shoes. "Good thing they're leather___ your feet should be dry in there," Seth said, trying to comfort her a little.

"That's true, but I didn't want to get them wet." She took a brush from her purse and started brushing her neck length, brunette hair. He handed her a cup of coffee as she applied mascara: high-lighting her hazel eyes.

"Thanks Seth." She checked herself in her pocket-sized mirror.

"I don't know why you waste your time with that stuff; you look breath-taking without it," he stated, taking a seat opposite her.

"Thanks, Seth. You are such a charmer," a blushing smile covered her face, "It's a girl thing; you won't understand." The door opened, and in came Tonya and Stephanie.

"Good morning Tonya; Steph," Seth greeted, followed suit by Cindy.

"Mornin' y'all," they replied as they took their umbrellas and leaned them in a corner.

Tonya walked over to the coffee machine and poured herself a cup, then reached for the cream to find it empty. "Shit," then turned to Seth asking, "Seth, can you reach up in the cabinet and bring down a can of cream?" He smiled and walked over to reach for the cream while Tonya quickly undressed him with her eyes; the others watched her, smiling in silence. Tonya was a young woman in her early thirties. She would not be considered drop-dead-gorgeous, but she was beautiful nevertheless, with big brown eyes, Indian looking cheekbones, and smooth dark skin.

"Hey, Seth, when are you getting your car back?" Cindy asked while putting away her cosmetic kit.

"I'm picking it up this afternoon."

Stephanie took the can from him saying, "Honey, the amount of money you make, you should have two vehicles." She handed the can to Tonya who poured a second cup for her co-worker. "Not too much sugar now; I'm too old to be getting diabetes." Stephanie was of African descent like Tonya but had struggled much through life, facing many prejudices in her youth. Her old fashion style of clothing had a motherly effect on the people around her. The door opened and in walked Michael, a young college student. He was about six feet tall with a knack for comedy; the way he walked and acted often inspired laughter in the people around him.

"Waz up my Nubian sister!" he said loudly, looking at Tonya and throwing his hands in the air.

"Waz up my European brotha," Tonya responded imitating his movements.

"Yo Tonya, that ain't funny___ I told you I'm from Da Bronx." His comical pretence to be offended caused them to laugh. "Mornin' Seth, Steph, Cindy." He hung his coat. They responded to his greeting in accord before he turned to Tonya again. She was still fixing coffee for

Stephanie and herself. “Yo, Tonya, how ‘bout hooking up a brother with a cup of black coffee___ two sugars.”

She looked at him in playful disgust. “Get your narrow butt over here and get it yourself; I ain’t your maid.”

“I ain’t know you checked out my butt already. So, how ‘bout them digits.” They laughed loudly as he made his way over and poured himself a cup.

“I don’t think so Mikey.” She sat beside Stephanie and handed her a cup.

“Well, I’m heading down to get started,” Seth informed as he stood up and walked to the door when Cindy called out to him.

“Hey, I’ll be down in a few to go over the relic they sent us last week. Those bastards in New York messed up the preservation process, so I had to re-do it.”

“You know where to find me.” He exited.

“Woowey, that brotha is all dat. If he asked, I would drop my draws right here,” Tonya remarked as she fanned herself. Stephanie looked in the direction of the door while Cindy responded in laughter.

“Girl, you are wild___ you act like you don’t see him everyday.”

“You wouldn’t go out on a date with him if he asked you?” Tonya asked Cindy as she took a sip of her coffee.

“Yes, I would; I just love his accent,” she replied, red in the face as she accentuated on love.

“His body ain’t bad either. If I was twenty years younger, I’d be ridin’ him like a race horse,” Stephanie added, sipping on her coffee.

"You so crazy," Tonya teased as she and Cindy giggled.

"I may be old, but my eyes ain't gone bad yet."

"He is well toned; I felt his arm this morning on the way in___ he must work out a lot more than he used to do," Cindy informed, leaning in towards Tonya.

"Girl, you lucky."

"Okay, y'all, just pretend that I'm not here," Michael remarked, pretending to be annoyed, "Y'all could show this brother some love too, you know."

They laughed as he sat down next to Cindy who gave him a hug and said playfully, "We love you too Mikey."

Tonya finished her coffee and threw the cup in the trash, then walked over to Michael and kissed him on his cheek asking, "You feel better, Mikey?"

He smiled saying, "I'm the man."

"That you are, Mikey," Cindy remarked as she got up to leave.

Tonya stopped at the door and turned to Stephanie. "Steph, let's get going and open up."

"I'm right behind you, love."

"Hey Mikey, when you done with the books in the back, I have a cart-full in the front to put on the shelves, so come up for it," Tonya informed him then turned and left with Stephanie right behind her.

"I'll be there, my Nubian sister," he flirted as he brushed his blonde hair from his face.

Four

Seth worked diligently at his computer translating ancient Latin to English. Piles of paper cluttered the desk around him from one end of the table to the next. Cindy walked in with some old, preserved parchments and rested them on the table beside him. “Seth, you need to clean up this mess.” She pulled some papers together in a neat pile. “What you working on?” she asked, resting her hands on his shoulders and looking at the screen.

“Some Roman documents. It looks like records from their Senate.” He leaned his head against her and looked up at her face. She pulled her hair behind her ear as she scanned the desk, then reached out and picked up a paper.

“What’s this? It looks like a poem.”

“It is___ go ahead and read it.” He continued typing, but she handed it to him instead saying, “You read it; I like to hear it read to me.” Seth took the paper and inhaled a deep breath, then started reading loudly:

The Memories

I remember a time not long ago
Of your enchanting smile and its gentle glow
Your comforting touch that held me close
Is what I seem to remember the most

When life had you down and you came to me
I was glad to be there—to set you free
But now that you're gone, I can't find meaning in life
No cure for this pain, this love, this strife

I pray every night as I look at the moon
That I would get to see and hold you soon
I've seen it each night as I promised I'd do
'Cause I'm sure that you're doing the same too

As time passes by from day to day
I still love you in every way
And as I write this little rhyme
I pray our love will meet in this time.

"Wow, that poet was really in love with that woman. Did you find it among those government documents you are translating?" she asked, taking the poem and looking it over.

"No, I wrote it sometime this week and forgot it here as usual." He got up and went to a nearby refrigerator for a grape juice.

"You wrote this?" Her tone was doubtful.

"Yes." He came back to his seat under her constant gaze of disbelief.

"The reason I ask___ is because you don't seem like the type that___ might have any interest in this sort of thing." She looked down at the paper again.

"Why would you think that?" he asked, interested in what her response would be.

"Well, the muscles and the way you have your hair pulled back in a pony tail___ your karate stuff. Don't get me wrong, you are a gentleman, but you just have that hard, play-boy look about you, you know?" She finished stumbling over her words as Seth laughed.

"So, although I'm nice, you're saying I don't show any emotions." He looked at her argumentatively with a mischievous smile on his face.

"No___ I don't know___ I guess those earrings in your ear give you that bad, pretty-boy look. This is not something that a bad boy would write." She realized that she put both feet in her mouth and then quickly changed the topic asking. "So who is she?"

"She was someone I knew." His tone was solemn.

"What do you mean by that?" she asked as she looked at the poem.

"She died some time back. She was the wife of a previous boss, but he use to beat on her. I taught her Latin at one time when we somehow fell in love. The most we ever did was kiss though, so don't give me that look." He could see a twinkle in her eyes as though she just found out about a juicy scandal.

"I'm sorry to hear that." He sat back in his chair, and she pulled a chair next to him. "So what are you referring to when you wrote 'I've seen it each night as I promised I'd do'?" She pointed to the line as he leaned over to look at it.

"Don't you have some work to do?"

"I'm on my break. Come on, Seth; show me that softer side you have hidden under that buff bod'," she teased.

"If you must know___ after I left the service of my boss, I told her to look at the moon for the comfort in knowing that I would be looking at it thinking about her___ I made a promise to look at the moon and think about her every night till the day I die." He took a drink under her gaze and smiling face.

"Aw… how sweet; do you still look at the moon and think about her?" She held the poem to her chest with a lover's touch as though the poem could somehow touch her heart the same way it was meant to for Nikkia.

"Yes___ I made a promise, but sometimes the moon don't show, so I look at a picture of one when it is not out." He reached for the poem, but she pulled away and asked.

"Can I make a copy of this?"

"Sure." She ran to the copier and made a copy then brought back the original.

"I still can't believe you wrote this."

He took a drink and asked, "You want me to prove it? I could write one right now."

"Prove it."

"Okay." He switched to a new page on his computer and started writing as Cindy stood behind him reading silently:

Picture Painted

I can picture you standing under a waterfall
As I picked up the phone to give you a call
Water falling from high above
Glistening your body my love

Drenching your hair so long and black
As a warm breeze blows across your back
Blossoms falling from the trees near by:
A picture so perfect I could cry

Green moss and bright flowers that make you smile
Keeps my head spinning for awhile
As you step from the fall, I imagine your grin
While the sun shines down on your tanned skin

(I held the phone as my mind ran wild)
The water splashing as you smile
Like a goddess, your beauty shine
I am happy to say you're mine

I thought for a moment on this theme
When the operator's voice shattered my dream
I reset the phone and dialed your number
Frowning, for the operator did encumber

You said hello across the line

Sending chills along my spine

My heart pounding to a voice so sweet

That I even felt it skip a beat.

To Cindy, from Seth with love.

"Well, what do you think now?" he asked as he leaned back satisfied that he proved his point.

"I…I don't… know what the say; …if I did not see it—." The poem held her attention in a way that she could not finish her statement as she looked at the computer screen.

"Well, it was inspired by you." He hit the print command and printed out a copy, and then he erased the window. "Here___ take it. I know some of it is kind of mushy, but I was caught up in the moment___ I hope you like it." She took it still spellbound.

"Wow, Seth."

"I hope I resolved that little stereotype you had about me. I can be sensitive too," he informed as she looked at the poem and started walking to the door.

"I have to get back to work." She left and closed the door behind her.

Five

Later that afternoon, Seth walked by a window and looked out. The sun shone brightly in the blue sky, erasing all traces that rain fell that morning except for the few drops found sprinkled on the flower petals and the leaves of the trees that bordered the roadways. He continued up to the front desk and stopped when he saw Tonya.

"Tonya!" he called out catching her attention as she checked out a number of books for a customer. He walked up to the counter and stood to one side.

"Hold on, I'll be right there, Seth."

"Take your time." He leaned back against the counter looking around at the variety of people, both young and old, walking around the library, while others sat reading in various locations.

"What's up?" she asked, walking over to where he stood.

He turned to her and replied with a smile on his face. "I'm about to go pickup my car. If Mr. Vincleburg calls, let him know."

"Okay." She walked back to her post to assist a customer. Seth turned and strolled in the direction of the lounge and entered. Stephanie sat resting her head on the newspaper she had opened on the table but did not move when the door opened.

"Hey, Steph, are you taking a late lunch? Don't mind me, just collecting my umbrella." He picked up his umbrella without paying much attention to her. He opened the door and closed it again without leaving, then turned slowly and started sneaking up on her. He grabbed her shoulders and shouted, "Boo!" but there was no response. Seth frowned worrisomely as he shook her saying, "Stephanie, wake up." He shook her again, but nothing happened. He ran to the phone hanging on the wall and dialed nine, one, one.

"Nine, one, one emergency, how can I help you?" came the voice of the operator.

"Hello, my name is Seth Lover from Richmond Public Library. My co-worker is unconscious in our lounge room. Please send an ambulance." He was as calm as possible, but his heart was racing like a chariot of ancient days.

"Is the patient breathing?"

"Hold on." He dashed over to Stephanie and placed his hand on her nose but he did not feel her breath, so he checked for a pulse, then rushed back. "No, she is not breathing and her pulse is weak," sounding a little bit excited.

"Do you know CPR?"

"Yes."

"Administer CPR until the medics arrive."

"Okay." He hung up the phone and immediately dialed an extension and waited as the phone rung twice.

"Hello; Cindy speaking…"

"Cindy—," he exclaimed as she cut him off.

"Oh, Seth, what do you want?"

"I just called an ambulance. Can you meet them out front and guide them to the lounge room? No time to explain." He quickly hung up the phone, rushed over to Stephanie, lifted her limp body off the chair, and laid her down on the table.

He looked around for something to place under her neck but did not see anything, so he took off his T-shirt and quickly rolled it into a wad before placing it under her at the rachis of her neck to tilt her head back. He opened her mouth to see if anything got lodged in her throat but did not see anything, so he placed his hand on her stomach just below her rib-cage and started pressing. "One, one hundred; two, one hundred; three one hundred…" after counting to fifteen, he stopped to check her breath, but did not feel anything, so he opened her mouth again and started to apply mouth-to-mouth resuscitation. The sound of a fire truck came closer followed by the sound of the ambulance, but Seth did not pay attention as he checked for her breath again: still no luck. He placed his hands on her stomach again as sweat poured from his body, and he started pumping. The door flew open as Cindy walked in and stopped in her tracks.

"Oh my God!" she gasped, resting her hands on her chest. The firemen entered the room with their equipment, but Seth did not pay any attention and continued to pump her abdomen.

"Okay, buddy, we'll take over from here," came the voice of one of the firemen. Seth stepped away so they could do their job and walked over to the sink.

Cindy came over to him and handed him some paper towels. "You're soaked." He looked down at his bare body to see the sweat pouring from his skin as he took the towel.

"Thanks, Cindy."

"What happened?" she asked as she took some of the paper and started drying his back.

"I came to get my umbrella, and she was just lying there. I tried to scare her, but she did not move___ so I called nine, one, one."

The medics soon entered the room and ran over to the table. Seth and Cindy turned to see what was going on as they opened a stretcher. They turned her to one side and slid the stretcher beside her. "One, two, three." They counted, then they heaved her onto it, while another medic pumped air into her lungs with her equipment. They quickly strapped her down and rolled her out.

One of the firemen picked up the T-shirt and tossed it to Seth saying, "Catch___ She'll pull through; she had a mild heart attack. You did a good job, friend."

He caught his shirt and quickly pulled it over his back as the firemen gathered their equipment and left. Seth started to straighten the table and the chairs while Cindy sat on the sofa. She looked frightened as tears fell from her eyes. He looked up and saw the tears, so he walked over and sat beside her, "Don't cry___ Everything will be fine." He consoled as he pulled her to him. She buried her face in his chest and cried for a while as he held her in silence. Memories flooded his mind as he remembered how Nikkia used to do the same thing. "Everything will be fine, Nikkia." He stroked her hair and then realized what he said. "Sorry___ I mean Cindy. I'm on my way to get my car; we could go down to the hospital to see her this evening."

After a moment, she pulled away saying, "Sorry, Seth, things like this bother me."

"It's okay." He handed her his handkerchief covered in make-up from earlier that day.

"Thanks." She dried her eyes, and then looked at his T-shirt saying with a little chuckle. "Oh, Seth, I'm sorry." He looked down at his T-shirt to see her make-up smeared on it as she tried to remove it.

"Don't worry about it," as he stood to leave, "Are you going to be okay?" he asked as he picked up his umbrella that fell under the table.

"I'll be fine. I'll just sit here for a few minutes." He brought her a cup of water and gave it to her, then he gently brushed her hair away from her face.

"That's the spirit." She smiled as he turned and left, closing the door behind him praying, "Thank you, Father, for guiding me back to the lunch room; I wished I still had the power to heal." He strolled to the front desk looking down at the carpet as he walked.

"Seth! Hold up!" Tonya called to him as she excused herself from her customer and came over to him. "What happened to Stephanie?" Her concern showed all over her face as she looked up at him.

"She had a heart attack but will pull through. Call her family and let them know what happened___ I'm going to get my car."

"As soon as I'm done with this line here," she said pointing to a growing line of people. She returned to the counter while Seth headed for the door.

He stopped and turned back to her calling out so she could hear,

"Tonya, I'm going over to the hospital later to see Steph. If you want, you can come___ Cindy is going too."

"Awright, I'm there!" She turned to her customer and apologized. "Excuse the interruption." Seth exited the building, tucking his shirt in his jeans with his umbrella swinging on his forearm.

Six

A black Corvette turned off Belvedere Avenue onto East Main Street. The gold-plated rims reflected light from the evening sun as VCU students looked at it from a nearby park. The dark glass faded from gold tint to a dark tint adding an aerodynamic effect to the already sporty car. It rolled down the street drawing attention from children walking up the street and from passers-by as they drove on their way about their business. It came to a stop in front of the library when the door opened. Seth stepped from the car and quickly closed the door to avoid the chance of it getting hit by a passing car, then he made his way into the library. He stopped at the front desk and called out to Samantha, a college student who worked the evening shift. "Good evening, Sam. Tonya left already?"

She looked over to Seth while scanning a book and replied, "No, she's in the back." She flipped her blonde hair to her back as he thanked her and made his way to the lounge room.

He opened the door and peeked in seeing Tonya and Cindy laughing and talking between themselves. "What's up ladies; y'all ready to go?"

Cindy grabbed the papers and stuffed them into her purse while Tonya answered, "Steph's son called and said that she is fine, but the doctors are keeping her over-night for observation and no visitors are allowed."

"Okay." He took a seat beside them and leaned back in his chair.

"So what y'all want to do this evening? I have my car, and it's Friday," he asked as he hooked his car key to his key chain.

"No can do___ I have a date," Tonya replied.

"With who?" Cindy asked curiously.

"With a fine chocolate brotha that come up in here during the week," a mischievous smile covered her face, "And since you two datin' now, three would be a crowd."

"What are you talking about Tonya?" Seth asked, and then turned to Cindy, "What is she talking about?"

"I showed her the poem you wrote for me."

"I ain't know you is a playa, Seth," Tonya teased, and then continued singing, "Seth got jungle fever, Cindy got jungle fever."

"Girl, you wild." Her face turned a little red as she smiled.

"Giiiirrrrl, when a man write something like that, it could only be love," Tonya taunted Cindy, then continued as Seth looked on with a smile on his face, "So, can I have a copy?"

"Get your own." Cindy teased her colleague as Seth sat back listening to the friendly test of wits.

"Tramp," Tonya reacted in the same spirit.

"Bitch."

"Pigeon."

"Ho," Cindy fired back.

"Y'all are bad," Seth jumped in, "Tonya, I will bring one from my collection for you on Monday."

"How much you have?" Cindy asked.

"About eighty."

"You goin' to publish them?" Tonya asked as she stood to her feet.

"Yes, I'm just fine-tuning them right now."

"Well good luck with that," she encouraged as she looked at her watch, and then continued, "Well tall, dark, and handsome must be waiting for me; since Cindy swiped you up, I guess Joey will have to do," she said to Seth as she patted him on his face. They laughed as she left.

"So what's up, Cindy, want to catch some dinner and a movie? My treat."

"Naw, I'll pass, but you could give me a ride home."

"Come on, let's go." He walked to the door. He was anxious for her to see his car. She stood and followed him out the door then ran back for her raincoat.

Seven

They walked out the front door as the sun started to set in shades of orange and red against the spring sky with ducks and birds flying overhead as a jet flew even higher, leaving a trail of exhaust behind. He pointed to the Corvette and said proudly, "There she is."

"You lying___ where is your Berretta?" She was doubtful, knowing that he joked from time to time.

"I traded it in and bought that bad boy." He walked up to it as she followed.

"Seth, stop playing." She was afraid that the owner would approach at any minute, angry that Seth was playing around the car.

He hit the button on his key-chain and the door unlocked, and he opened it saying and waving her in, "Your chariot awaits, my lady." She smiled as he held the door open and then climbed in. She was still not sure that it was his but trusted him. He walked around the car and climbed in, then started the engine.

"Come on, Seth___ Whose car is this?" she asked as she ran her hands along the black leather seat, "I don't think you make that kind of money at this job."

"Remember two years ago I spent most of my money on stocks?"

"Yes." She remembered some years ago how he was broke all the time because he was throwing all his money in the stock market.

"Well, last year I sold them all, along with some other stock I inherited___ right around the summer___ and continued working on my second house on Franklin Street___ since I rented out the one I was living in."

"No, shit!" she exclaimed, realizing that his returns were good. "I didn't know you moved into the house on Franklin," her pride in his success caused her to reflect on her resent, bittersweet successes.

"Well, I had some money leftover to buy this car, but I waited to get it used. I found this baby about a month ago and traded in the Berretta___ but I wanted to add some features to it like this supped up engine and this sound system, not to mention the custom rims and tint." He turned on the radio to ninety-eight point one. "Listen to that baby pound___ real smooth."

"It's nice___ I wish I could inherit a shit-load of money."

"I still have to manage the money though. The house is bringing in some money from the tenants, and since the market is low, I am re-investing and buying stocks cheap." He could not tell her his secret that he was immortal and changed identities several times, passing on his property to himself and that he worked for thirty years to get what he had.

"I make enough to pay for my house, and I have a few dollars saved, and a car I can't drive." She turned up the volume a little on the radio.

"Why do you catch the bus? What's wrong with the car?" He changed gears and sped up a little.

"The car is fine___ I just don't know how to drive."

"You bought a car and can't drive?" His curiosity peaked as he checked his blind spot and changed lanes.

"Yeah, I bought the thing a few months ago so my good for nothing ex. can drive me around to get groceries and go out___ stuff like that___ but he was a real jealous type with a touch of violence, so I had to dump his ass___ that sounds silly, huh?"

"Well at least you got rid of him," he replied as he slipped a CD into the deck asking, "You like Chicago?"

"Some of their music is good," she reflected on his age, "Aren't you a bit young for this kind of music? I thought you would be listening to rap or something."

"Nope, the older music have melody; anyway, as I was saying___ at least you got rid of him."

She breathed a sign of relief. "It wasn't easy; I had to put a restraining order on him. He beat the hell out of a date I had about a month or so ago, and he still comes around thinking he could get back with me."

"You'd think he'd be in jail after he beat up your date." He stopped at a light and looked over to her almost melancholy face.

"He did, but not for long. He spent two weeks in the slammer, and he is back out again bothering the hell out of me." She observed the change in the light. "Your light's green." He pulled out with a slight screech.

"What does the cops say?" he asked as he changed gears.

"Not much. He leaves before they get there. They have a warrant for his arrest, but they can't seem to find him; his grand-parents got money, so he always have somewhere to go." She paused and looked at him with a smile on her face. "Look at me rambling on about my problems; sorry to bore you like this."

"Don't be silly; you are not boring me; at least you are getting it off your chest."

"Well, thanks for listening." She looked around as though she was missing something. "You got any more CDs?'

"Yes, they're behind your seat___ just in front of the sub-woofer." She took off her seatbelt and looked behind her seat.

"You took out your back seat?" She pulled out a case from between her seat and the sub-woofer, where the back seat used to be.

"It was the only way I could fit the fifteen-inch sub and the amps; I have a sub in the back there with four mid-range speakers resting on the amps___ And on the doors I have one mid-range and two tweeters."

"Now all you're missing is a CD changer." She buckled herself back in.

"I have a fifty disk changer in the trunk, but I haven't read the manual yet." He turned onto Monument Street.

"Where do you live again?"

"I can't believe you forgot," flipping through the CDs.

"It's up near Horse Pin road."

"That's right___ I remember now. You can't blame me; I've only been there a few times."

She flipped the leaves of stored CDs and stopped at one, saying ecstatically, "You got Prince? I love him."

"It's not Prince anymore; it's symbol man."

"Please; he'll always be known as Prince." She pulled out *The Gold Experience* CD while ejecting Chicago and slid in the new selection.

"Play number four and number seven; I like the 'Shhh' song and that 'beautiful woman one' too." They rolled along on the almost empty road. She selected the song and turned up the volume a little as they listened in silence until she forwarded to number seven. Both, in unison, started singing it in horrible falsetto as he turned onto her street. The sound was mellow as Seth downshifted and slowed his ride to twenty-five miles an hour. Up ahead, Cindy spotted a car in front of her house and inquired to herself.

"Who the hell is that?"

Eight

A man adjusted himself in the driver's seat. To Cindy's horror, it was her ex.

"Dammit!" she shouted. Seth lowered the music as he pulled into her driveway behind her blue *Kia*.

"Fuck! Fuck! Fuck!" Her rage increased at the discomfort of her ex's presence. "I can't believe this is happening to me," she grumbled as her face turned red.

"Hold on," Seth said, and he got out of the car and came around to her side. He opened her door and took her hand. She exited, infuriated as her ex jumped out his car.

"What the fuck do you want, Steve!? Get the hell away from my house!" Steve stood at six feet tall and was fairly built. He looked about twenty-nine with long, sandy blond hair and a short beard that gave him a rustic look.

"You were in love with that man?" Seth asked as he closed the door.

"Yeah, I was a fool." She threw her purse over her shoulder.

"I see you found yourself a rich nigger," Steve insulted as he slammed his door and walked over.

Seth knew the word and smiled, stating to Cindy, "He's not really bright. What did you see in him?" She didn't answer as he followed her to the other side.

Steve reached out to grab her, but she pulled away. "Don't touch me!"

"Come here, bitch. You belong to me." His sinister tone caused Seth to step forward, but Cindy stopped him.

"No, Seth, I can handle this." Neighbors came to their windows and observed while others stood in their yards watching. Seth leaned against his car as Cindy shouted, "Get the hell off my property, Steve!"

"You whore! Fucking niggers now?" A few young African Americans heard the statement and started walking over with their white friends close behind.

"What the fuck that white boy say? He lookin' to get a beat down," one of them declared as they all agreed. Steve reached out to grab her again, but she jumped back. He swung at her without warning, but missed her face as she jumped back against Seth, who caught her.

"That's enough, sir," Seth warned pulling Cindy behind him as she trembled at the eluded slap. It was so close that if she did not take that extra step back, he would have floored her.

"What you want, nigger? I'll beat your black ass!"

"Are you crazy?"

"I'll kill you for fucking my woman!" his tone more menacing than before—Seth could smell alcohol on Steve's breath.

"We are co-workers, sir, I'm just giving her a ride home," Seth replied trying to calm the man down.

"Fuck you," Steve responded and reached out, trying to grab Cindy from behind Seth.

Seth pushed him back saying, “I cannot in good conscience allow you to do that, sir___ She does not desire your company.”

“The nigger can speak fucking English. I’ll change that.” He saw the make-up stains on his shirt and flew into a hysterical rage—saying as he swung at Seth, “You fucking nigger.” Seth caught his arm and broke it as he followed through with a knee to Steve’s head, breaking his nose.

“Kick his ass!” the young men shouted, while a few neighbors called the police.

Seth pushed him away saying, “Sir, you do not know me, or my abilities. Please stop this.”

Steve’s rage consumed him as he responded, “No nigger can beat me.” He swung with his left—his rage consuming his pain as Seth grabbed his hand. Tears rolled down Cindy’s eyes at the site. Seth moved Steve’s arm to the other side of his body as he turned and brought his foot against Steve’s left knee—breaking it. Seth once again pushed him away to the sound of sirens pulling into the neighborhood. Steve bled on the un-kept lawn as Seth walked over to Cindy and then turned back to Steve saying, “Even if she was the love of my life, you couldn’t take her away from me.” He hugged her as the police came up with drawn guns.

One of them walked up to Steve, and then called on his radio for an ambulance. Cindy released her death grip on Seth and called to the officer who came over to them. “Officer, that man lying on the ground there was my ex-boyfriend. There is a warrant out for his arrest.” Another cop came up and handcuffed Seth as he wiped the blood off his hands on his shirt.

“What the fuck are you doing!?” Cindy shouted to the police, “Seth protected me when Steve tried to hit me."

The boys told another officer saying, "Yeah, that white boy swung at the brotha y'all got handcuffed over-there."

"Five 'O' always trying to arrest a brotha," another stated sarcastically.

A few neighbors came out backing up the young men, so they released Seth after a few more interviews saying, "Sorry 'bout the confusion, sir." The officer handed him his wallet and car keys as another asked, "Would you like to press charges, sir?"

"No, it would be a waste of money and time; besides, he will never be able to walk on that leg again. That's enough punishment that will last him a lifetime. His right arm is severely broken too, so I doubt he could do any damage___ even if the doctors repair it." He walked back to Cindy, who finished giving her statement.

"First Steph, and now this. How much shit can happen in one day?" she exclaimed as he sat down beside her, looking down at his shirt.

"This shirt's been through hell today," Seth muttered—he bumped against her. She buried her face in her hands as the ambulance pulled up.

"Hey, Cindy, they're taking him to Saint Mary's." She looked up—the crowd still gathered—embarrassing her even more.

"Hey, want to catch that dinner and movie?" he asked pulling her to him.

"Sure, let's go."

He stood up and made his way to an officer. "Do you need us for anything else sir?"

"No, we have all the information___ you can go."

"My co-worker is a little embarrassed. Could you have that car moved so I could take her to get something to eat___ or do you still need her?"

"She can go. I'm sure she needs to get away from this crowd," the officer agreed. Seth thanked the officer and walked back to Cindy.

"Let's go." He led her to the car and held the door open for her, while an officer moved the police car blocking the driveway. Seth jumped in, started the engine, and slowly backed out of the driveway. He threw the car into first gear and drove off under the evening sun.

Nine

Seth drove down Monument Avenue with Cindy at his side as the sun set over the display of white and pink blossoms from the trees that decorated the island dividing the flow of traffic. Vehicles of all makes and models packed the streets to a steady roll of about forty five miles an hour as people, young and old, made their way to their dates, or just to have a wild party with friends and family.

"Mind if I stop by my house for a quick shower? My clothes is a mess." She popped in a Kenny G. C.D.

"We could do that; I need to use the bathroom," she responded with a giggle.

"Hey, did you know I played the saxophone?' They drove past Willow Lawn Shopping Center where people were going shopping.

"No way!" Her response could not fool him to believe that she was not thinking about the unfortunate incident that just unfolded.

"Yep, but I'm not as good as Kenny G. here."

"I don't think anybody's as good as Kenny G." She leaned back in the black leather seat as he turned onto Malvern, made his way up the street, and then took a left turn two blocks up onto Franklin Street.

"Which one is it?" She looked around. "Man, this is a wide street."

"It's that one over there with the four pillars." He showed her, pointing to it.

"That's a nice place you got there." He made a U-turn, pulled up in front his home, and jumped out.

"Hold on, let me get the door for you." She smiled as she followed him with her eyes. He came around, opened the door, took her hand, and helped her out of the low car.

"You are such the gentleman. How is it you're not married yet, Seth, or have a girlfriend?" They walked up the steps unto the porch that extended the full width of the house.

"Well, I have not met the girl of my dreams yet," his usual mischievous smile covered his face as he teased, "But I'm hoping it would be you."

"Stop playing." She nudged him playfully, looking around the porch as he opened the storm door and inner door. "I love what you did with the yard; those shrubs look great," she stated after looking at the landscaping.

"Yeah, the landscapers did a good job. Wait till you see the back." He opened the door and held it for her.

"Hey, Seth, where did you get those furniture?" She pointed to one side of the porch.

He smiled proudly and walked over to the furniture. "I made them; hold on, let me hit the lights so you could see the details." He quickly turned on the porch lights from a dim glow to a bright one. "Take a look at that." He led her over to a sitting area on one side and pointed to a love seat made out of wrougth iron in the shape of an angel praying, with its outspread wings coming around to form the hand rest and back rest, while another pair of wings extended up and out to give it a three-dimensional look. The seat was made of wood and fastened with bolts, ending neatly against the wings that formed the front legs at its tips. Two other chairs of the same likeness, except for the second pair of wings, help surround a center table set on a pedestal with two cherubim hugging it.

"This is my favorite piece out here." He ran his hand over the table.

"This is really good. Where did you do the work?"

"I had a work shop in the basement of the other house, but it's here now in the basement." He proceeded to lift compartments on the table. "Check this out." He lifted the top that extended and slid over the love seat. "This way I can bring my laptop out and work on my writing when the weather is nice." He slid out another compartment on either side of the table that gave it a wider capacity and also slid over the love seat as Cindy watched in admiration, not to the detail of the table but to his enthusiasm. "I can rest my drinks and snacks on this side and still have room on the other side for my references, or whatever else."

"You are really talented, Seth. Did you do the details on the wings too?" she asked pointing at the feathers.

"No, a friend of mine did the work on that. I don't have the space or equipment to do it."

"Why do you have it in that dull red paint?" she asked, running her fingers along it.

"Oh___ it is not finished yet. I'm saving to have them dipped in anodized brass—that way it could stay out all year round." He closed up the table.

"Check the other side out." His excitement showed as he pulled her over to the other side to a brightly shined table. Four angels stood in the corners forming the legs, while a glass rested on top. "Now this here, I had made because I don't know how to do molding yet."

"Where are the chairs?" she asked, admiring the work.

"I haven't made those yet; I usually roll the angel chairs over."

She looked over to the chairs in amazement. "They have wheels?"

"Yes, they slide up and lock." His smile was bright with pride. "I did the inside first, this porch and the windows are the last thing left to do." He opened the front door. "I'm having four angels made out of marble to replace those wood pillars there, and then I will replace those railings with something similar to the table."

"Well, it sure has that Roman look." She entered the house as he held the door open.

"It is suppose to have that Greek effect, but the Romans adopted so much of the Greek culture that they look similar." He closed the door behind him bumping into her. "Sorry."

She looked around at the highly decorated setting as he closed the door. "Let me give you the tour." He turned on the lights, revealing a massive room to the right.

"Wow, this is real nice Seth; I see you went with an oriental setting here."

"Yeah, I had the wall that was dividing the hallway from this room removed to make it look bigger, and that same friend made the imperial dragon with the design I gave him to give that section of the house support. You can't see it, but it's welded to steel beams on the floor and ceiling that is running the length of the house."

"Is that brass like what you plan to do outside?" she asked walking under the dragon to the living room and running her fingers on the glittering dragon.

"No, I had it gold plated."

"That must have cost a pretty penny. How much money did you make in the stock market?"

"Yes, it did, but since I did the furniture myself, I had the funds to do it. Besides, my friend got it done cheaper than usual." He avoided answering her question and was glad she did not pursue it.

He followed her into the room as she looked up at the dragon again and pointed almost shocked. "Seth, your ceiling is cracking where the dragon meet it."

He looked up and smiled. "Naw, that's an effect to make it look like a lot of weight is on the dragon; look at its claws pressing against the ceiling," he pointed, "You see how the claws are digging into the woodwork there?"

"Yes."

"Well there are steel beams running there too. I had this place gutted and hired a contractor to re-enforce the structure, re-do the electrical work, plumbing, and to highly insulate this place, because I hate the cold."

"How long did the contractor take to do the work?"

"It took about seven months to do the work; I already had the ideas for what I wanted, and the money to do the work, so it did not take long. A lot of sub-contracting took place to get it done because I wanted to move in fast."

She looked around, seeing a huge oriental rug with a serpent design on it covering the room and stopping about two feet from the walls to reveal the hardwood floor. She turned to him and asked, smiling and pointing at the rug, "Is this custom?"

"Yes, mostly everything in the house is custom."

"It's soft," she stated before looking at the sofa near the front window with a love seat directly opposite that divided the living room from a small office, with a row of sliding windows exposing the back corner of the house. "Man, this is nice." She admired his house, soon forgetting about her previous encounter. "I love the way you have those cats as the hand-rest on the sofa and loveseat___ and those two chairs flanking the fireplace."

"They are leopards actually." His smile was wide and bright as he stood back looking at her as she examined the place.

"What are those tigers made of?" She pointed to the center table showing two tigers circling for a fight with fierce looks of death on their faces and red glass eyes as a glass top completed the top.

"That's made with silver; I think the strips are made from onyx. The two cranes above the fireplace are made from silver too." He pointed at the birds standing with open wings on the shelf above the gas fireplace.

"Those lamps are exquisite," she commented, looking at the tall, oriental style lamps that border the four corners of the room. She walked over to the office and looked out the windows at the last rays of sun being captured by darkness, then at the oriental style desk decorated with paintings and adorned with a computer system.

"I designed that office, but a contractor did the work. With work and all, I did not have the time to do it myself." He guided her out of the room. "Come on, let me show you the rest of the house." He pointed to the steps as they made their way to the left side of the house saying, "The room we just left, the steps, and the hallway upstairs have that oriental look. See the carpet leading up?"

She looked at a gray carpet with two dragons leading up the steps, with a stained glass scene of an oriental county-side hanging on the wall, and the handrail complimented with an etching of different martial art poses on glass, framed in brass. "You don't have children coming here much, huh?" noticing the fragile decorations. "You must love the Orient."

"It's the kungfu I do, I guess. The dragon, the cranes, the leopards, the snakes, and the tigers you saw behind us depict that form I do, but each room is different."

They entered the next room that glittered from the light coming from the living room. "Close your eyes." She closed her eyes with a pleasant smile on her face.

"What's the surprise?"

"You'll see." He turned on the lights to reveal a breath-taking site. A crystal chandelier hung in the center of the room with a brass dome covering the ceiling and corners of the walls in leaves and flower designs. A silver and gold curtain hung over the front window, bordered by two crystallized, European styled, dragons. To the right, the brass design divided the dining room from the kitchen with a beaded curtain of crystals in the middle flanked by sleeping dragons. In the center of the room stood a majestic table made from a fallen tree with a glass top, and, hanging from the corners of the ceiling were shrubs, adding a green luster to the magical out-door scene. Six chairs of similar design as the table surrounded it with long backs, inlaid with leafy looking fabric. On the floor, laid a brown area rug, decorated with designs of dry leaves and sticks, that added it's own flavor to the room.

"Okay, open your eyes."

"Wow, this is nice." She looked around the room impressed at the work.

"The lights change color too___ and it also dims," he stated and demonstrated with the knobs on the wall.

"This place is like a palace."

"I designed it to look like a heavenly garden, with mystical European dragons."

"It's nice."

"There was a wall where those two stone dragons are, but I had it removed to make more space. Those brass-covered pillars of leaves separating the kitchen from this room are supporting the weight of the rooms upstairs with the aid of a steel beam that runs above it and down on either side." He walked over to the kitchen, and she followed. "Instead of the walls, I had this short wall made just behind the dragons and placed these marble tops on top to use like a counter."

She looked to the right at a counter with a small bar just behind it, then to the left at the other counter as they past through the beaded curtain to the kitchen.

"I see___ you eat on this side," she remarked noticing stools under the counter.

"Yes." The kitchen was modern, with a stove and oven, microwave, refrigerator, cabinets, and a little inlet for the pantry on the left corner of the kitchen.

"Would you like something to drink?" He took a glass from a cabinet above the sink.

"I'll have some water, thanks." She looked in at the room beyond the kitchen. He stuck the glass under the refrigerator dispenser then gave it to her as she rested her purse on the counter.

"This room back here is the den," he pointed out, leading her into the room and hitting the lights after giving her the water. A sixty-inch, high-resolution television lined the wall between the doors leading to the kitchen and the hallway. Two recliners stood in the middle of the room with a glass face cabinet filled with electronics hanging above the television. "I built that cabinet and the casing that goes around the TV with the speakers built into the walls and ceiling." They exited the room to the living room.

"I'll be right back, let me go shower and change," he said looking at the time.

"Hurry up. It is almost seven." He dashed up the steps and quickly returned as he pulled a clean black T-shirt over his body with a lightweight, black, leather jacket in his hands.

"Let's go!" he called as he turned off the lights in the kitchen and dining room. He walked into the hallway and turned off the living room lights, then he returned and held the front door open for her as she came from the half bath next to the den.

"You have a nice place here, Seth." She exited, and he closed the door behind them.

Ten

Later that night, about seven-thirty, Seth and Cindy sat eating at a café in Cary-town. People came and went, while others sat with their girlfriends and boyfriends enjoying each other's company. Cars drove by as neighborhood kids roamed the streets after a week of school.

"I didn't know the balcony seats were open to the public," Cindy commented over a half finished beer.

"This will be my first time sitting up there," Seth added as he drank an orange juice.

"So, Seth, you trying to get me drunk? How come you ain't having one with me?" She knew he did not drink when he had to drive and wanted to tease him.

He looked at her straight-face and then rubbed his chin as though deep in thought about the idea. "That's not a bad idea, drink some more." He laughed at her annoyed expression continuing, "I have to drive, and your life is in my hands when I'm behind the wheel tonight." He took another swig. "I couldn't, in all my power___ let anything happen to you tonight."

"Why not?" The dim lights reflect off her hazel eyes in sparkles of brown and green.

"Because you are my date tonight," he replied as a waiter cleared the table.

"So, how is this date supposed to end?" A mischievous smile

covered her face while she looked around when a man walked through the café selling roses.

"I don't know, but it will start with some flowers." He signaled for the man to come over. "A dozen roses for my date please."

"What colors, sir?"

"Three yellow ones for friendship; two orange ones for warmth; those three bluish ones for romance; three white ones for passion; and one red one for love." She smiled and blushed under his constant gaze.

"That will be twenty-four dollars sir." The peddler handed Cindy the flowers while Seth paid, and then he went on his way to peddle his goods.

"Are you always this charming with the ladies?" Her ever-present smile captivated him; he was glad she was enjoying herself. She noticed women walking by and looking at the bundle in her arms, causing her to blush even more.

"I don't go out on dates too often, so when I do, I tend to go overboard. I hope it pleases you."

"You are too much, Seth; no, it's not too much. Thanks."

He paid the waiter for the meal and stood taking her hand and helping her up while a young lady, observing from her seat with her girlfriends, shouted out, "You go, girl. Hold on to that brotha; ooh, 'cause he fine—hmm, hmm, hmm."

They laughed, while another of her friends told her, "Girl, leave those people alone."

"Goodnight, ladies," Seth replied with a bow, and then he took

Cindy's arm and walked out of the café. He exaggerated his motion to embarrass Cindy beyond her already frazzled state.

"Aren't I the special one." If she could smile any wider, her lips would split.

"Well, you are, and I want you to have a great time with me so you could never say Seth is a jerk." His feminine imitation of a woman's posture made her laugh as she smacked him gently on his back.

"You are crazy."

"What time is it?" He looked at his watch. "It's twenty minutes before eight. You want to go in now, or do you want to put those in the car?" pointing at the flowers.

"Let's put them in the car. I don't want people staring me down and plotting to steal you from me tonight." She laughed as he guided her to the parking lot behind the Byrd Theatre.

"Seth, thanks for treating me tonight; after this evening and with Stephanie, this is really nice." He opened the door for her to put the flowers on the passenger seat.

"I am glad to do it, Cindy; it is not every day a guy gets to take out a beautiful young woman such as yourself," he thought he could have helped her forget the awful incident, but was glad that she was happy with him, "Don't sit on those when I take you home; they have thorns in them."

"You are such a flatterer, Seth." She blushed as he closed the door.

"I meant every word; flattery don't get people anywhere for long." He took her arm in his and started walking back to Cary Street saying, "You are a beautiful woman, like I told you this morning. I'm just use to you so I don't feel embarrassed to tell you so."

"Well, thanks for the compliment." They rounded the corner to an already forming line.

"Fifteen minutes to eight," he muttered looking at his watch. The line moved slowly as people handed their tickets to the attendant.

They finally got to the attendant, but upon seeing the tickets, he said, "Give those to the lady at the steps." They walked over to the steps and handed the attendant the tickets.

"Enjoy the show." The attendant's warm smile caused them to smile wider.

"Thanks," they replied, when Seth stopped and asked, "Do you want anything for the movie, like pop-corn or a soda."

"No thanks, I'm stuffed." They climbed the steps and found a couple of seats near the front.

"So___ have you seen *Shakespeare In Love*?" he asked when they sat down.

"Yeah, but I liked it; I don't mind seeing it again."

"I saw it too___ It's a good concept." He stopped short and looked at the beautifully lit chandeliers, which she noticed.

"These look just like the one in your dining room."

"Yes, this is where I got the idea from." There was a pause. "This place is beautiful, and since you are beautiful, I thought what could be better than to bring two beautiful creations together." She giggled to his flirtatious comment.

"I hope the organist plays tonight before the show."

"That would be nice." He leaned back in his chair and pretended to stretch as he deliberately and animatedly threw his arm around her playfully. "I always wanted to try that."

Later that night, couples came pouring out of the theater and scattered in different directions. Among the crowd, came Cindy and Seth as they made their way to the other side of Cary Street. "Where are we going now?"

"There is an ice-cream parlor right up here; I thought you might be ready for dessert," he replied.

"Man, I have not had ice-cream in a while." She hugged herself as a sudden chill hit her. Seth noticed, so he took off his jacket, placed it around her, and brought her to a halt.

"Slide your hands in the sleeves." She did, and he hooked the zipper and zipped it up to her neck saying, "Don't want you catching a cold now."

"But now you will be cold," she complained.

"It is a little chilly, but the shop is right up the street and I have a shirt in the car. So I'll be fine."

They continued to the shop and entered as people followed behind, while others left or sat at tables. They made their way to the front and stood to the side looking at the menu, while others ordered.

"So what do you want?" he asked, nudging her a little.

"I don't know, you already done so much already."

He looked at her and said, pretending to be stern, "Look woman, didn't I tell you that I want you to enjoy yourself?" He paused and answered his own question, "I guess I did not. Well, get anything you want, and stop trying to ruin my buzz." He tried to hold a serious face, but her smile broke his concentration.

"Okay, Seth, I want a chocolate sundae with rainbow sprinkles and a cherry."

They called a lady over, and Cindy ordered her sundae.

"What would you be having?" she asked him as the lady waited.

"I want a strawberry cone, dipped in chocolate sprinkles, with a cherry on top," he told the lady who gave him a price, which he paid. She returned with the sundae and his change, then left and came back with his cone.

"Thanks." He followed Cindy to a table.

"So who's Nikkia?" she asked as they took their seats.

"What?" Hearing the name surprised him.

"Who is Nikkia? You called me that earlier today." She eyed his shocked expression as she dug into her sundae.

He took a moment and replied teasingly, "Oh, I did call you that by mistake when you were bawling down the place back in the lounge."

"I was not bawling." Her assertion was convincing to no one, "Mmm, this is so good."

"She was that woman I told you about." His thoughts reflected on Nikkia and the evenings they spent under the shade of the tree.

"Oh, so that moment we had brought back some memories?" She attacked her sundae, shoving spoonfuls in her mouth.

"Yes___ I used to hold her as she cried under a tree in a meadow on her property. We used to meet there in the evenings and study Latin until the setting sun and singing birds distracted us."

"How romantic. It's a wonder you are not married or have a girl yet."

"Well, the right girl has not come along yet." He did not see the ring God promised him he'll see and continued after taking a lick of ice cream, "I am patient though."

"So how old are you? If you don't mind me asking."

"I'm twenty-five."

"No way!" Her jaw almost dropped at the revelation.

"I knew you were young, wow." She looked at him doubtfully, "The way you carry yourself, I thought you were about twenty eight___ let me see your license." Her demand was met as he whipped it out and showed her.

"Wow, you are twenty-five. Your parents must have been wealthy."

"I did inherit a lot of money at a young age___ and was able to acquire a master's degree in linguistics___ particularly in Latin and Greek; I could see how this could make me seem a lot older than I really am," he explained as he took a few bites from his cone, "How old are you?" His motive was to change the subject so he would not continue lying about himself.

She finished up her sundae and replied, "I'm twenty-eight; man I can't believe…" She looked at the license again, and then gave it back. He pocketed it and finished up his cone.

"It must be the muscles because you do joke around some." She paused a little, reflecting. "That means you've been working at the library since you were twenty one?"

"Yes." He stood and took her empty bowl and discarded it before walking out into the chilly air.

"Yes___ I could see it now___ you must age well because you still look the same as you did four years ago; look at me and all these lines on my face."

"Don't beat-up yourself; you look great___ So tell me about yourself," another attempt to change the subject, as they walked to the car.

"Well, I was born and raised here in Richmond. I wanted to become an Archeologist but found myself working in preservation instead of actually going out on digs, got a job at the library preserving documents, and almost married a total jerk. That about sums it up," she replied as they got to the car.

He opened the door for her and closed it when she sat down before making his way to the trunk and opened it. He pulled out a crumpled shirt, threw it over his shoulders, then shut the trunk and entered the car. "Did you sit on the flowers?"

"No, I pushed them to the side; see?" she replied as she picked them up in her arms.

"They are pretty." He started the car and pulled out of the parking lot to Kenny G's C.D.

Eleven

Seth and Cindy rolled down the street near Thomas Jefferson High School on Malvern Avenue when Seth broke the silence. "Ah, I want to see something while I'm passing by." He pulled into the back of the school and stopped in the parking lot; then he looked up at a full moon for a moment as Cindy stated almost dreamily.

"It's beautiful isn't it. You thinking about Nikkia?"

"Yes, I am. She lives in my memory."

"Well, I kept my promise," he muttered to himself, grabbing the C.D. holder, opening it, and flipping through the leaves till he came to a Backstreet Boys C.D. He popped out Kenny G. and slid it into the case, and quickly jumped out of the car as Cindy watched him with a puzzled look on her face.

"What you doing?" He opened her door and leaned over, sliding the Backstreet Boys C.D. into the player. He turned it to number eight, and then stood up asking with his hand outstretched, "May I have this dance under this moonlight?" She smiled and took his hand, and he pulled her out after she laid the flowers on the seat. They embraced each other, and they moved on the parking lot under the moon to the beat of the song: she, leaning against his chest as he held her closely.

After a moment, he lifted her eyes to his, as the song changed to number nine, to see a glimmer of tears. He smiled as they maintained eye contact while her hair blew across her face under the soft, night breeze. He slowly bushed it away from her face as she once again laid her head against his shoulders. He felt her tears soaking through his shirt, so he asked in a soft voice, "What's the matter?"

"Oh, nothing."

"Are you sure?" He held her firmly in his arms, thinking of means and ways to comfort her, but came up empty.

"I've never been on a date like this before, and all that have been happening with Steve___ I just feel comfortable crying when I'm with you. I feel that you would not judge me." He listened intently and realized that all he had to do was listen. "I guess that is why you make such a good friend."

He lifted her face off his shoulder and looked into her teary eyes. "That is why I'm here to comfort you as your friend, to help you get it all out." He smiled, looking into her eyes as she held him. Her face slowly moved towards his, and her lips parted.

He brushed her hair. "Cindy, I would love to, but we work together. Don't let this moment cause something we will regret tomorrow." He could kick himself for refusing but remembered his covenant with God.

She smiled as she laid her head on his shoulder again. "You are right."

The tenth song came on as they held each other without dancing. She stopped sobbing and pulled away, so he released her from his grip. He pulled out his handkerchief and gently dried her eyes before she picked up her roses and sat down. He closed the door and jumped in behind the wheel. She smiled and said when he pulled away from the school, "I guess that beer really did a number on me."

"Naw, that should have worn off by now." He turned onto Monument Avenue. She turned off the music and sat silently as he drove.

"Did you have a good night tonight?" he asked, breaking the silence. His mind wondered about what her kiss would have felt like but was broken by the sound of her voice.

"Yes, you are an excellent date."

"I'm glad I was able to give you a memorable evening."

"That you did, Seth, that you did." A smile covered her face as she thought about the wonderful evening she had.

He pulled onto her street, slowly turned into her driveway, and stopped. He jumped out and opened the door for her, helping her out. He closed the door and walked her to her house as she handed him the flowers so she could fish in her purse for her keys. Her hands were a little shaky, so he took the keys and opened the door for her.

"Well, good night, Cindy." He handed her the keys and flowers. An expression of fear came over her face as she took off his jacket. "What's the matter?"

Twelve

She looked down at the floor red-faced. “After this afternoon, I’m a little frightened to be here by myself tonight.”

“Well, you don’t have to worry about Steve; I broke his arm and leg.” His smile was reassuring, but he realized it did not lift the fear she had.

“I hate to do this, but could you stay until I fall asleep? I promise to be good.” Her embarrassed smile softened him as he looked at her, almost in tears, before turning to see Steve’s car still parked on the street.

“Hold on.” He ran over to his car, turned off the ignition, and then returned, closing the door behind him.

“This place hasn’t changed much since I was here last,” he commented, looking around at the cozy setting.

“I finished the upstairs and had a deck put in out back___ other than that___ nothing has changed.” She placed the flowers in a vase and added water to it before resting it on the dining-room table. “If you want anything, just help yourself. The kitchen is still the same way it was about a year ago.” She made her way to the bathroom. He walked into the small kitchen and found a glass in the cabinet after his third try. He filled it with tap water, then walked over to the back door and looked out at the massive yard and the new deck as he quenched his thirst, and then returned to the living room to look for the television.

“Cindy! Where is your TV now!?” He returned to the kitchen and put the glass in the sink.

She stepped out from the bathroom in her nightgown and answered pointing to her bedroom. "It's in my room above the bed," and walked back into the bathroom. He strolled past and saw her removing her make-up before he made a right turn into her room.

"I see you got that flat-screen mounted on the ceiling!"

"Yeah! That way I could turn into a vegetable on the weekends!"

He turned it on and flipped the channels to the news; then, he leaned back on the soft pillows. Cindy came in after a few minutes looking around.

"You missing something?" He sat up on the bed and followed her with his eyes.

"Yes, I guess Muffy must be upstairs," she answered climbing in beside him and getting under the covers.

"You still have that crazy cat?" he asked as he looked up at the television and lowered the volume.

"Yeah, she's bigger now though." She found a comfortable position facing him.

"So how come you stop coming over?" she asked after a moment of silence.

"I've been busy with the house, and you were dating at the time. I guess our schedules conflicted." She smiled, not at his reply, but because he was there with her. She felt protected and safe, "If I was not here now, I'd probably be home working on the chairs for the porch table or fine-tuning my collection of poetry for publishing." He smiled at her lovingly, hoping that her fear was subdued so he could leave. He felt the tension of lust tempting every fiber of his being and was afraid of making a mistake that could doom him for the rest of his life.

"You are such a work-a-holic." Her teasing remark countered his zeal as she pulled the covers up to her neck. He pulled a pillow from under his head and swung playfully at her, but she quickly pulled the cover over her head to shield the blow as they laughed.

"Since you completed the deck, which looks great by the way, now all you have to do is learn to drive," he fired back with a little nudge. She swung a pillow at him in response. "Is the car insured and up to date with the state?"

"Yes it is."

"What about your learner's permit?" He placed the pillow back under his head and leaned back, muting the television.

"That is good too. I renewed it because Steve was going to teach me the practical part that you started before you got tied up in your house." She looked up at the television, distracted by the program.

"We'll start back Monday. It is time you learn to drive."

"Recite a poem for me___ I like the one you gave me today, but I want to hear another one. I can't believe we've worked together for years, and it is now I'm finding out a lot more about you than I ever did before." She looked across at him with a smile.

"Well, we only hung out about two months before our schedules started conflicting, so I guess we are picking up where we left off." He looked over to her and saw her expectation for a poem. He did not want to do one because his already tense desire might climax into a catastrophic lost.

"Let me think of one that is not mushy," he muttered to himself.

"But I like the mushy ones," she insisted. He took a deep breath, rested his head against the pillow, and started reciting:

This Friendship

I'm sharing my appreciation for who you are
Your finesse and ambition surpassing o'r star
In the short time we've known each other
We've shared o'r dreams without a bother

Thank-you for your smile so sweet
That captures me whenever we meet
Let's hope this lasts forever more:
The friendship in us like never before

You've touched my life in a positive way
And there are no words for what I'd like to say
I hope I've been a good friend to you
By supporting you in the things you want to do

As last year came to an end
I had hoped happiness would be yours my friend

While this friendship grows with time
My soul has flown through this rhyme

He fell silent as she looked at him with a smile on her face saying, "That was great, thanks for the poem." She patted him on his chest, and then rolled over—away from him—and closed her eyes saying, "When I fall asleep, you could leave, and I'll be fine."

"I will. I'll watch some cartoons in the mean time," he replied as he flipped the channel to the Cartoon Network, feeling the surge of emotions under her touch. "*What power do women have, that their very touch could cause a man to defy God Himself*," he thought. "*Am I such a primate that her gentle touch of affection would arouse millenniums of desire*?" His mind seemed to focus on his excitement, just being next to her. "*I must be in control___ I do not love her. ___Why am I trying to justify lust?*" His passion ran hot…

Seth woke up the next morning, saw the television hanging from the ceiling, and realized that he fell asleep. He tried to get up but felt suppressed and unable to move. He looked down to find Cindy's leg and arm wrapped around him as she drooled on his chest, with his arm wrapped around her shoulders pinning him down. She moved, slightly adjusting her body on him as she took deep breaths, looking peaceful as she snuggled on him, sending forbidden sensations through his body, which he managed to control by focusing his full attention on the cartoon. However, he could not deny the hardness in his crotch. A few minutes passed when he felt a movement at his feet and looked down to see Muffy curled up at his feet and purring softly. He smiled and leaned his head back against the pillow and watched the cartoon until Cindy opened her eyes.

"Good morning," he greeted, giving her a little squeeze.

"Mornin'; did I pin you down?"

"No, I fell asleep." Muffy came over to her, and she petted her for a few seconds when Seth stated, "Well, I'd better get going because my breath could probably melt steel, and I'm hungry." He sat up and tucked his shirt into his pants while she adjusted herself.

"There is some Listerine in the bathroom, and if you give me a few minutes, I'll make us some breakfast." He stood up and made his way to the bathroom, then returned shortly as she sat at the edge of the bed gazing into space. She finally stood and opened the blinds, letting the sunlight flood in; then she made her way to the bathroom as he struggled with the tension building in his loins.

They sat down to breakfast in the small dining area with a spectacular view of the backyard, with flowers bordering the fence.

"This is good; I have not had breakfast cooked for me in a long time," he complimented as he dug into the fried eggs and toast.

"I'm glad you like it." She was looking at the flowers he gave her. "So what are you doing today?" she asked after a few minutes.

"I think I will do my laundry, then do some work around the house. What do you plan to do today?"

"My mother is coming over; she wants to have a family re-union in the backyard sometime in the summer," she added as she finished her meal.

"Sounds like fun." He finished his eggs and drank the milk.

"Yeah right. First she will complain that I am not married, then she will try to set me up with some crazy guy as always."

Seth laughed as he gathered his plate and utensils and made his way to the kitchen. "Well, I'd better get going. Thanks for breakfast; it was delicious." He threw on his jacket and made his way to the door. She followed behind him and waved goodbye as he pulled out of the driveway and disappeared down the street.

Thirteen

One year passed and Cindy eventually got her license, after driving Seth to and from work. Her confidence improved, and she was ready to drive by herself without Seth's guidance at her side. Stephanie recovered, but had the watch her diet and activity level. Tonya got engaged but did not plan to marry anytime soon. And Seth decided to resign so he could concentrate on his writing, but he still maintained contact with his former co-workers, including Michael, who worked on the weekends by helping Seth around the house for a little extra cash. Seth sat in his backyard, where he built a small deck that wrapped around from the back door on one side of his house to the basement door on the other side. An in-ground pool lined the right side of the property from Franklin Street, between the back of the house and the two-car garage. He sat under an umbrella typing on his computer and sipping on some lemonade while the hot summer breeze blew across his sweaty neck and the birds dipped in a water hole on the far end of the yard, chirping loudly as they flew back and forth from nearby trees, while squirrels chased each other around, or dug for food in the freshly watered lawn. The sound of the doorbell broke his concentration as it rang loudly, so he stopped and made his way around the house to the front to see Michael and his girlfriend, Cathy, standing on the porch looking in.

"Over here!" he called to them.

They turned and smiled as Michael called out, "What's up, Seth? Thanks for letting us have a pool party in your back yard."

"What's happening, Cathy, you still with this bomb?" She smiled at his teasing comment.

"Yes, he still makes me laugh."

"Mikey, bring the car round back so you can off-load your stuff," Seth told him as he took Cathy's arm and walked round to the back of the house. "I'll take care of this lovely lady for you." They walked round back where Seth poured her a glass of lemonade, asking as Michael pulled up to the back gate and started off-loading the drinks and music, "Are you graduating too?"

"No, I have one more year to go." She was a junior at the Virginia Commonwealth University. Her outgoing personality and hardworking ethics impressed Seth, who was glad that Michael was fortunate enough to have met her.

"Hey Cathy, come give me a hand, will ya?" Michael called, straining with a box. His lanky body crouched under the weight of the box and his strained facial expression was enough to make Seth and Cathy laugh.

Seth went down to assist him saying, "I told you, you should be working out."

"Hurry up, Seth." His voice gave a sign of urgency as he brought up his knee to try and support the weight of the box.

Seth grabbed one end of the box and helped him carry it to the deck, while Cathy pulled a sign out of her purse and went round front to hang it. She returned to find Seth typing away while Michael was firing up the grill that stood over at one corner of the deck.

"I heard you graduated with a Ph.D. when you were twenty-one," Cathy stated, sitting down at the table.

Seth saved his document and turned off the computer replying, "Yes___ I was fortunate to have wealth so I did not have to work while I was in school."

"So you studied hard? ___And here I thought you were just smart," Michael teased as he slapped some burgers on the grill.

Seth stated, "Hey Mikey, the basement door is open so you and your grubby friends can use the bathroom down there." He was not about to have fifty drunken people run through his place: for fear of the destruction of his fragile decorations.

Cathy took a drink, smiling as Michael grabbed a beer from a cooler beside him and opened it, spilling it all over his shirt. They laughed as she stated between breaths, "The beer is still hot silly, and y'all shook the cooler when y'all brought it up."

"I got some shirts in the dryer," Seth informed as he poured himself some more lemonade, laughing at his friend. Michael walked around the corner taking off his wet shirt, before disappearing inside the house.

"So you are like, twenty-seven or something?" Cathy asked, going over and checking the fire.

"I'll be twenty six in August."

"I thought you were older___ the way Mikey usually talk about you, but I didn't think you look old at all." She flipped a few burgers, inhaling the delicious smell.

Cars started pulling into the alley and stopped there with young men and women jumping out, bringing food and beverages. Cathy introduced them as Michael came out wearing a T-shirt. The chatter filled the air as more arrived from the front. Michael worked the grill, while Seth entered the house and set his computer on a recliner in the den then went back outside. Cindy came round back with her new boyfriend, congratulated Michael on his graduation, and upon seeing Seth, came over. "Hey, Seth. I want you to meet Tom; he's a Lawyer."

Seth shook his hand as Tom greeted, "I've heard a lot about you."

"I hope it's all good things," he replied with a smile, and then turned to Cathy and called out, "Hey, Cathy! ___Toss a couple beers over here for Cindy and Tom!" She brought the beer over and was introduced to Tom. Then she left to mingle with her friends.

"Where's Tonya and Robby?" Seth asked, between the splashing and shouting.

"They should be here soon," Cindy replied, drinking the beer and looking around at the people jumping in the pool, or eating Michael's burnt hamburgers.

"I saw your book, Seth," Tom stated.

"Did you like it?"

"You must be a real ladies man." Tom's tease brought a smile on their faces as Seth reflected on his temptation about a year ago with Cindy.

"Nope___ just have a God given gift to write," he replied, looking over to see Tonya and her fiancé coming into the back yard. "Tonya! ___ Over here!" She smiled and came over with Robby at her heals.

"What's up my Nubian sister!?" Michael shouted, throwing up his arms as he came over from the grill to greet her.

She hugged him and congratulated him, and then pointed to the grill. "You burning something."

He turned to see smoke rising. "Oh shit," and ran over to it, while they laughed at his unfortunate clumsiness.

The party continued into the early evening as some drank and made merry in the pool, and others sat around chatting. Seth and Cindy conversed with Tonya and Robby while Tom pulled the car into the back, when Seth heard a familiar voice.

"Well, see you around Seth, me and Tom are going home to relax a little." She gave him a hug, "Don't do anything I wouldn't do." He squeezed her in his arms, but his thought was on the familiar voice he heard. He released her and watched her jog off before turning his attention to the direction where he thought he heard the familiar voice, and made his way through the crowd, after excusing himself from Tonya and Robby.

He heard the voice saying as he got closer, "Sorry Cathy, I had to work."

"I know how it is." He came into their view to see Cathy hugging her friend.

"*Nikkia? It can't be.*" The thought flooded his mind at the sound of the familiar voice as he walked over, but he stopped short when he beheld the young woman. She was about his height with long blonde hair and bright green eyes, complimented by dimples as she smiled. He found her to be very beautiful as she looked around the yard.

He turned to walk away when she spoke again asking Cathy, "Where's Mikey?" Seth stopped and turned again to the sound of her voice to see Cathy pointing in the direction where Michael was chatting with his friends. The girl left Cathy and went over to where Michael stood while Seth approached asking, "Who's that?" He pointed over to the young woman as Cathy followed his gaze with her eyes.

"Oh, that's my cousin Veronica; she's a junior at the University of Richmond." Seth kept his stare on Veronica. Cathy noticed his interest and teased, "I see, you got a thing for her."

He looked down at her and replied awkwardly, "She reminds me of someone—at least her voice does."

"Hmm, I see," and called out, "Hey Veronica! ___Come over here___ there's someone I'd like you to meet!" She smiled, showing her dimples, and came over. "Veronica, I want you to meet Seth, the poet."

"Hey, nice to meet you," she greeted, taking his hands, "So you wrote that collection of poetry that Mikey used to seduce Cathy. What was the book called?"

He gazed into her green eyes—admiring her alluring beauty. "It's called Passion Within: A Touch of Emotions," he replied. Thoughts flooded his mind to intoxication, trying to make sense of the unusual turn of events.

"He did not seduce me___ although the poems did soften me up," Cathy declared with a smile.

"I read some of them and thought they were good," Veronica

complimented as Cathy excused herself to get a beer.

"Thanks." His state of shock revealed an outward facial expression at the uncanny similarity of her voice.

"Is everything alright?" she asked as she flipped her hair over her shoulder.

"Yes___ it's your voice, it reminds me of someone," he quickly changed the subject by asking, "What are you studying at the University of Richmond?"

"I'm majoring in Criminal Law." Cathy came back with a beer and handed it to her.

"No thanks, I got to hit the gym in a little while before I head back to the dorm." She pushed the beer away.

"You and Seth are the same; he doesn't drink much either." She opened it and took a drink.

"*Could it be she?*" he thought to himself as he looked at her and then to Cathy as they talked.

After a brief moment, Veronica said to Cathy, "Well, I have to run; I'll see you at the graduation party next week," and then turned to Seth, "It was nice meeting you."

He took her hands, never taking his gaze from her green eyes. "The pleasure is mine." She waved at Michael and left as Seth followed her with his eyes.

"Earth to Seth," Cathy teased, "She has that effect on men; I'm surprise she don't have a boyfriend yet." He looked into space as flashbacks of him and Nikkia flooded his mind—of them sitting under the tree and the day he kissed her goodbye after winning his freedom.

Fourteen

Later, the crowd grew thin as the night overshadowed the scene. Seth, Michael, and Cathy cleaned up the place with a few stragglers. The night air blew the scent of pine from the pine trees that inhabited a vacant lot in the alley, while the moon shone brightly in the night. He looked up at the moon and thought about Nikkia—then about Veronica's voice and spunky strides. Michael came over to him and broke his thought saying, "Seth, I'll come by tomorrow and clean the pool. See you later." He picked up the trash bag and dumped it in the trashcan, with Cathy on his arm, while Seth entered the house and locked all the doors with his thoughts wondering, his mind searching for an answer to a question that didn't exist.

After an hour of pacing back and forth, he sat down, turned on his computer, and started writing:

Could It Be You

Could it be you? My love to be
The only one who could set me free
That voice so familiar in my mind
Could this be a divine sign?

I pray that it's you after all these years
The one to finally end my tears
I will do my best to see if it's you

So I can finally have a love that's true

I don't know what I'll do or say
But I pray that God will guide my way
The moment is here when time seems to stand still
As I think of you with all my mind and will.

His fingers typed the words as they poured from his heart, followed by the tears from his eyes that ran down his cheeks and onto his shirt. His heart ached with a yearning and a hoping that this might be her; the love he could have in this time. After a moment of just looking at the screen, he dried the tears that blinded his vision, made his way to his room, plopped down on the bed, and removed his clothes before lying down.

After staring at the ceiling, he opened his mouth praying: "Dear God, it has been a long time since I've been here, and today, I heard a promising sign. I ask for your blessing as I take action in finding out about Veronica and hope that she is the one. I did not see the ring you told me I'd see and hope she has it. Thank you, Lord, in Jesus name. Amen." He closed his eyes to try and sleep, but he tossed and turned for hours before finally dosing off.

The next day Seth awoke to the sound of a small racket in the back yard and looked out the window to see Michael and Cathy cleaning up the yard. He took a quick shower and changed before going down stairs and out to the back yard.

"Good morning, you two!" he called out to them as they raked up the cups and paper plates they missed the night before.

"What's up Seth," Michael greeted, "I see we missed a shit-load of trash last night."

Cathy held a bag open while he dumped the trash in. "Seth, you coming to the graduation, right?"

He stood up and stretched. "I'll be there for the party, but I won't be able to make the ceremony."

"That's okay, not too many people will be there for the ceremony, but the party will be hype," Michael stated.

Cathy added, "Don't forget to dress up. Mikey's mom haven't seen you since you published, and she's dying to congratulate you."

"The dress code is formal___ my family is making a big deal out of this graduation since I am the last child to graduate," Michael informed as he took off his shirt and jumped into the pool.

"Is it cold?" Seth asked, looking over the railing.

"No, I turned on the heat earlier___ it cleans better when the water is warm." He swam around in the water. Cathy handed him the scrub-brush and the cleaners as Seth came down and took the trash to the trashcan.

"Seth, are you bringing a date to the party?" she asked as she sat down on the deck looking at him coming back. She handed him the T-shirt Michael used yesterday as he sat down beside her.

"No." He stretched again, leaning back in the chair.

Michael looked up from the pool and commented, "Hey Seth, come to think of it, I never see you with no woman around here___ What's up?"

"I haven't met anyone that really interest me," he replied with a smile, "And Cathy here is already taken."

"Stop playing, Seth, you could have any girl you wanted 'cause you're rich, young, well built, and you are quite poetic," she stated.

"Thanks for the compliment." He looked up at the sunny sky.

"Hey Seth, why don't you take Veronica? She doesn't have a date, and doesn't really want to drive," Cathy suggested after a moment of silence. She reached for her purse and pulled out a pen and a book, "Here's her number; give her a call."

He took the number saying, "Y'all won't give this a rest, huh?" He was quite glad to get her number but felt it would be best to play the cool bachelor role.

"Nope," she replied with a smile, "I know you like her, so give it a shot."

He stood up and went into the house; then, a few minutes later, he returned with a tray of orange juice.

"So what did she say?" Cathy asked as he set the tray down on the table.

"She said she would love for me to be her escort, but she is moving this weekend, so she will have to call me back with her address." He tried keeping a straight face and succeeded. He was not only happy to have this beautiful date, but was also glad to get the chance he needed to see if she was the one.

"Good for you, Seth, now we all have dates," Cathy stated, taking a glass of juice to Michael.

"Hold on, I said I was her escort; a date is different."

"You are such a stiff… yet charming at the same time," she called back to him.

"Yo, don't forget I'm your man now," Michael jumped in. They laughed at the joke and his comical gesture.

"You know there's no other man for me but you." She kissed him and returned to the deck with the empty glass. "I forgot she was moving."

After a few hours passed, and the cleaning was completed, they parted company with Michael saying, "See you at the party next week."

Fifteen

Later that day, Seth pulled up and parked in front his house and hurried in with his gym bag. He dropped it at the front door and walked briskly to check his answering machine, but there wasn't any messages. He took up the phone and walked over to the next room and fired up his laptop. He sat there looking at the screen before starting to type but soon stopped as he looked at the phone, hoping Veronica would call. After a moment, he continued writing into the night before shutting down and going to bed. He repeated this routine for three days without hearing from her, so he started to get worried. He dialed her number but realized that her number would be different since she moved. His mind raced on every scenario, each not making any sense as he squeezed the phone in his hand. Once again, he closed is eyes in disappointment.

Early Wednesday morning the phone rang. He looked up at the clock to see six minutes past five. "Who could be calling at this hour?" He picked up the receiver saying, "Good morning, Seth speaking."

"Hello, Seth, sorry for calling so early; it's the only time I had all week," came Veronica's voice over the phone. A smile covered his face as he sat up, livelier.

"No need to apologize… I'm glad you called," his thoughts focused on her voice because he made a mental note not to make the mistake of calling her Nikkia, "Where are you? You sound like you're on the street."

"Yes, actually, I'm about to go to work, but the phone at home is not hooked up yet, so I stopped at a pay-phone," her voice rang sweetly in his ear, "You have a pen and paper handy?"

"Hold on." He opened the drawer to his night table and pulled out a pad and pen. He was frustrated that he could not get the pen and paper fast enough. "I'm ready." He took down her address and hung up soon after that. He stared at the address for a few minutes and then lay down again and gazed at the ceiling with a smile on his face.

Saturday afternoon came, finally to Seth's impatience. His car shone brightly from being washed and polished earlier that day, and the interior had a touch of jasmine scented freshener. He loaded the C.D. changer with a variety of soft music and fine-tuned the sound output. He checked his wristwatch to see it was seventeen minutes past three as he put away the car cleaners. After inspecting the car, he smiled and then hurried down the street to a neighborhood barber shop to have his ends clipped. He then came back about an hour later to shower and change for the evening's event. He greeted a few neighbors on the way up the street on their way out, then entered his house with a skip and a jump. After a long shower of scrubbing and soaping himself—about three times—and brushing his teeth several times, he dried himself and applied lotion to his body then flexed his toned muscles in the mirror before leaving the bathroom. He entered one of the upstairs rooms, which he had turned into a walk-in closet, and quickly slid on his under-garments. He checked himself in the mirror again, smiling all the time; then, he splashed on a little cologne before putting on a suit he picked up from the dry-cleaners the day before. He slid on a pair of black, lose-fit pants, then a dark-blue, oriental style top that he tucked neatly into his pants before zipping it up and fastening it at the waist. His excitement seemed almost unbearable as he wrapped his belt around his waist before lathering his hair with extra gel. He combed it back into a smooth sheen and tied it into a ponytail as he checked in the mirrors for any lose hair, which he smoothed down. He returned to the bathroom, washed is hands from the gel, and then applied a little more cream before returning to the room. He opened a drawer, pulled out a wooden box where he kept his jewelry, and carefully slid on a gold, imperial dragon bracelet that spiraled around his right hand, locking with its claws for a firm hold. After securing the dragon, he attached a gold bracelet that looked like a leaping tiger to his left fore-arm that also fastened with its claws as the tail wrapped around the forearm for a firmer hold. He slid the sleeves over the bracelets, then pulled up the left sleeve again and snapped on a gold watch that hung loosely on the wrist. He took out a chain bracelet that matched the watch, but hesitated before he finally snapped it on his right hand. He stood in front the mirror, moving around to see how his jewelry looked, and being satisfied, he slipped on an onyx engraved ring on his right pinky and a gold ring, similar to the one he gave to Kimbi's son, on the next finger. He pulled his black, double-breasted, sporty jacket on, smiled in the mirror again, and then slipped on his highly polished shoes before leaving the room.

He came down the steps, entered the kitchen, and retrieved a long-stemmed rose that had light-yellow petals with red trim. Humming a little tune as he picked up his keys, he locked the door behind him and jumped into his car. He carefully placed the rose on the passenger seat as he sat and let the car idle for a bit. After a minute or so, he pulled out the address from his wallet to double-check it then drove off to meet Veronica.

Sixteen

The car glittered as he drove west on Patterson Avenue and made a U-turn to the opposite side, coming to a stop in front a house a few blocks away from a nearby Jewish private school. He placed the rose on the dash, smiled, exited the car, made his way up the walkway, and then rang the bell. He stood there looking around as he heard footsteps coming towards him. A young lady opened the door with a smile saying, "Come in, Veronica will be ready soon."

"Good evening," he greeted as he entered the house.

"Sorry about the mess, we haven't finished unpacking yet."

"It is quite alright," he assured her as she showed him to a seat, then turned shouting.

"Veronica! Your date's here!" She turned back to him and smiled, before excusing herself as Veronica shouted back, "LaWanda! Come give me a hand!"

He waited for a few minutes before LaWanda came out saying, "She'll be out shortly."

The door opened, and another young lady walked in wearing a waitress uniform saying upon seeing him, "Hi."

"Sandy… this is Seth, that writer Michael kept getting them poems from. He's taking Veronica to the party tonight," LaWanda introduced from the kitchen as he stood to shake Sandy's hand.

"Oh, we found out where Mikey got the lyrics when he got us to buy the book," Sandy informed. "Your work is good. Do you mind signing it for me?"

"Thank you. I'd love to sign it for you." She excused herself.

"Are you and Sandy going to the party too?" he asked La Wanda, who was leaning against the kitchen door. Sandy returned with the book.

"We'll stop by later." He signed the book and handed it back to Sandy as Veronica entered the cluttered room.

"Sorry to keep you waiting, Seth."

He stood to his feet as LaWanda shouted and snapped her fingers. "Work that dress girl!" She spun around in a circle as they admired her. She wore a cream, thin-strapped satin dress that wrapped to the front and came down to her ankles, with a slit coming up about mid-thigh on her left leg to reveal flesh-tone stockings. Her matching shoes wrapped elegantly around her ankles as she stood completed with a matching purse. Her dyed dark-brown hair, with a lighter shade of high-lights, flowed down to the middle of her back.

"You look absolutely stunning, Veronica," Seth complimented as she smiled, revealing those dimples while the overhead light reflected off her green eyes. He wanted to swallow her tongue and hold her in his arms but knew how wrong that was just thinking about it.

"I'm ready," she stated, looking at him. He walked to the door and held it open as Sandy came up behind. He took her arm in his and escorted her to the car while Sandy and LaWanda watched him unlock the door and help her in before closing it and making his way to the driver's side.

"Hold on!" she gasped, rolling down the window and shouting

to LaWanda over the roar of the super-charged engine, "Hey, LaWanda, I forgot my chain on the dresser! Can you get it for me please!?" LaWanda disappeared and came back carrying the chain.

"Thanks, girl. My father would kill me if I did not have this on." She fastened it and pulled—the ring—around front. Veronica rolled the window up as her friend returned to the house and then continued, "My father gave me this last year saying it was very old." She held the ring in her hand, and he looked at it. His heart wanted to leap out of his chest at the sight of it.

"It's nice," he revved the engine, "It looks like this ring I'm wearing." He showed her his ring and smiled as her eyes widened.

"Wow___ This is wild," a surprised smile covered her face, "Where did you get it?"

He pulled out from the curb and headed down the road answering, "I inherited it about five years ago," and pointed to the flower, "I bought that flower for you; I hope you like it."

"Thanks___ It's beautiful." She picked up the rose and took a sniff of the fragrant petals while his mind raced, trying to control his excitement. She smelled the flower with a smile on her face. Her bright-green eyes glowed as she looked at him saying, "Nice car. What year is it?"

"Thanks, it's a two thousand model___ with some custom work." He nervously changed gears.

"I see you like to listen to soft music." She looked at him with a smile.

"I like a variety, but I did not know what you'd like, so I burned a few slow CDs for tonight." He smiled nervously, still thinking about the ring.

"You didn't have to go through all that trouble," she stated, brushing her hair from her face.

"It was no trouble." He changed gears again as he overtook a car. He tried hard to control his nervous reaction to the sudden turn of events. "What is your heritage? If you don't mind me asking." He wanted to be sure that this was not a trick sent to test him.

"My grandfather___ on my father's side___ is from China, but he is mixed with Indian I think. And my grandmother is English and African blood. When you see my father, you would not think he was mix with all those things because he looks Indian."

"American Indian or India Indian?"

"India Indian." She daintily pulled her hair around her ear. "On my mother's side, they are Irish and German mix; she has piercing blue eyes." He listened to her sweet voice that tempted him to reach over and embrace her, but he knew she was not Nikkia and controlled his primitive desire. "I don't know how I ended up with green eyes."

"They look pretty on you."

"Thanks. So where are you from?" He could feel her eyes on him and imagined her smiling face and her attractive dimples.

"I lived on an island called Trinidad for a while." His heart was still pondering if she was Nikkia or someone else. Her voice is of Nikkia, but she looked so different. He thought for a moment on the ring, and then on her, and realized that he could love her without regret. They conversed about many things on their way to the party, with his joy only growing stronger as they talked.

Seventeen

They arrived to find the party in full swing, with Cathy and Michael making the rounds to mingle with family and friends. Veronica pointed out her parents and excused herself, while Seth walked over to where Cindy, Tom, Tonya, and Robby sat.

"Hey, Seth, who's the girl?" Cindy asked as he hugged her, then Tonya. He shook Robbie and Tom's hand.

"That's Cathy's cousin."

"She's pretty hot," Tonya commented as Robby agreed. She smacked Robby playfully. "You're not supposed to agree with me." They laughed as Seth leaned over to Cindy, following Veronica with his eyes.

"She's the one."

"What makes you think so?" She followed his gaze to Veronica.

"Somehow, I know." He watched Veronica walk around the room, mingling with her family with a captivating smile. Her graceful strides compelled confidence as her brilliant smile captured his moment. Her bright eyes seemed focused. Her satin dress flowed as she danced with her father to *Unchained Melody*, while her mother watched from a nearby table. Seth spotted Michael sitting with Cathy and his mother, excused himself, and made his way to where they sat.

"Good night, Mrs. Tolanski, how are you doing?" he greeted Michael's mother. She looked up and smiled, expressing her joy to see him.

"Seth, how have you been? I bought a copy of that book you wrote and just loved it." She squeezed him with a motherly love.

"I'm glad you like it, Mrs. Tolanski."

"How is it you don't come over anymore?" she asked as he sat down beside her.

"It's been busy; I'm working on my next book and doing research at the library." She listened intently with a smile. "And when I'm not doing that, I'm working on my house."

"So is the book making any money?"

"Not as much as I'd hope, but at least I made my initial investment back. A few song writers are looking at turning some of them into songs, so I expect some more money to come in."

"Well, I'm glad for you." He excused himself with his thanks and turned to Michael and handed him an envelope.

"I little something." Michael thanked him as he took the envelope and opened it, looked at the check, and muttered to himself.

"A thousand dollars."

"That is not for the fine job you did in school; it is for a dance with your girlfriend here."

They laughed when Michael responded, "For another grand, you could take her home for the night." She playfully smacked him across the head. He put the check in his pocket as a song came on.

"Shall we dance, Cathy?" Seth asked, taking her hand.

They moved onto the dance floor; Cathy complimenting, "You look really nice tonight, Seth."

"Thanks___ you look great too." He immediately dipped her before spinning her around the room. They danced around the floor—she, holding him tightly, not knowing what would come next.

"He's good," Tom stated.

Tonya added, "That's an understatement." The song ended shortly after and he escorted her back to her table.

"Show off," Michael taunted, taking Cathy's hand and leading her back to the dance floor.

"You were great. How 'bout another dance later?" she asked almost teasing Michael.

"Sure," he replied as he looked around for Veronica. "Where did Veronica go?" he asked no one in particular.

"I thought I saw her go out on the patio." Michael answered, pointing him in the direction. Seth excused himself and made his way to the balcony. It over-looked a lake with a wooded background. He saw Veronica leaning against the marble banister.

"Is everything okay?" he asked as he came up to her. He looked up to see the brightly shining moon and leaned against the banister beside her.

"Everything's fine___ I just needed to get some air." She looked up at the moon with a smile on her face. "The moon looks lovely tonight."

"It sure does, but it could never be compared to your beauty." She laughed as they looked up.

"Are you always like this?" Her eyes fell on him as she waited for his answer. She remembered his earlier compliment at the house and those he made on the ride over. He smiled for a moment in silence when she nudged him.

"Most of the time I am." He faced her with a smile, almost bashful that he really was like that.

"What am I thinking? Of course you are; you write poetry." She remembered his book and some of the words she read from it.

"How is it you don't have a girlfriend?"

"Well, I've been waiting for the right girl," and asked, "How is it you don't have a boyfriend?" She thought for a moment. He, admired her with awe.

"Well, I've been busy with school and have not met anyone that really tickled my fancy." A song caught his attention as it started playing.

"That's the *Don Juan DeMarco* song. Did you see the movie?"

"No, didn't really have the time."

"Do you have the time to have this dance with me?" he asked, reaching out his hand. She looked at him and smiled inquisitively.

"Right here?"

"Yes, what better place to dance with you than under this full moon atop this balcony?" He took her hands in his and guided her to the middle of the balcony.

"I am not as good a dancer as you are," she warned as he pulled her close. She held him around his neck while they danced to the beat of the song, brushing their cheeks together. After a moment, he pulled slightly away from her, gazing into her eyes.

"What?" she asked with a smile.

"I just wanted to capture this moment___ the way the lights reflect dimly off your eyes in glimmers of green." Her smile widened as they embraced again, "I hope that does not freak you out."

"Not at all. I'm not used to so much detailed attention but not at all."

The fragrance of her hair tickled his nostrils as it mixed with her perfume while they danced slowly around the balcony. He looked up at the moon and smiled, a warm breeze blowing gently across the balcony as her hands ran along his back. With every motion, her touch sent waves of emotions through his body as he held her firmly.

"You are dancing great," he finally complimented, trying to harness his mind that swirled with every gesture of motion—from every breath that brushed across his neck—from her warmth that seemed to dance with his soul.

"Thanks. Just don't swirl me around."

"How about one dip at the end?"

"I'll try that." A few moments pass before the song came to an end.

"Ready?" He held her tighter.

"Yes." He rounded his hand on her small waist while his other hand danced up her back. He dipped her slowly, then brought her up, and locked eyes for a moment with smiles before parting from the dance.

"Damn song! Why did it have to be so short?" He was genuinely upset that the song came to an end so quickly but expressed himself more playfully to hide his true feelings from her.

"Poor baby___ I'll save one more just for you," she teased and patted him lightly on his face as they made their way into the hall. He touched his face where she patted him and absorbed the sensation of her touch but was careful not to appear over eager.

Seth drove down the street with Veronica at his side—she leaning back in the comfortable seat. The car rolled slowly on the empty road with an occasional car flying by. She looked over at him and said with a smile, "It would seem that you are trying to keep me to yourself as long as possible."

"Maybe a little." He picked up the pace a little bit and then turned to her and asked as the soft music caressed their ear lobes. "Is that better?"

"Yes."

"So where do you work?" he asked.

"I have a summer job over at Leroy's Donut House," covering her mouth and yawning, "I have to be in for six in the morning."

He looked across at her, just remembering something, "You know what? You owe me a dance; I just remembered."

"One day I'll make good on my word."

He turned onto Patterson Avenue and finally stopped in front her place. "LaWanda and Sandy aren't back yet," she stated, looking to the spot where La Wanda normally parked. "LaWanda's car isn't here."

"They'll probably be along soon," he assured as he stopped the car saying, "Wait one second." He jumped out the car and made his way around to her. He opened the door and helped her out as she held her purse and the flower in her hand. He quickly closed the door before escorting her to her door, and he waited till she opened it.

"Thanks for being my date tonight," she said softly, capturing him with her undying beauty and hegemonic smile.

"The pleasure was mine," he replied with a slight bow, and he quickly turned, making his way back to his car. He heard the door close behind him. As he reached his car, he heard the door open again.

Veronica ran out shouting, "Seth, hold up!"

"What's the matter?" He was concerned that something was wrong and hurried back to her.

"Can you help me with this zip?" she asked, trying to reach it. He smiled that his fear was premature and stood behind her taking the zipper and sliding it down just enough for her to grab it, admiring her blemish-less skin.

"There you go."

"Thanks again, Seth." She closed the door once again as he made his way to his car, fired it up, and drove off.

Eighteen

Veronica walked into the lounge room of her workplace when her shift came to an end and she sat down drinking a *Sunny Delight* orange juice. The door opened. A co-worker walked in with a dozen roses and a smile on her face. "Jen, your boyfriend sent you flowers?" Veronica asked, looking at them. She enviously admired the lustrous colors of roses but was happy to see Jennifer smiling happily.

"No, girl, these just came for you." She was surprise and wondered who could have sent her the bouquet as Jennifer handed them to her. Jennifer stood back asking anxiously, "Who's it from?"

"I don't know." She was happy to receive it and admired the bright petals, still bewildered that it was hers.

"Girl, open the envelope and see," Jennifer pushed, pointing to the envelope stuck to the arrangement. Veronica opened the envelope and took out the paper. "Well, what does it say?" Jennifer asked, looking over Veronica's shoulder and reading along with her:

> Dear Veronica:
>
> How are you doing? I hope all is well with you. I want to take this time to thank you for that memorable dance Saturday night. I really don't know how else to ask this, so I wrote this poem instead:

Hello Lady

Hello lady; take my hand
Music'll play by a live band
The atmosphere'll be mellow for this dance
When you grace the floor for instance

We'll join o'r bodies across the dance floor
Enjoying each other—letting o'r hearts soar
You could look into my eyes—at my soul
Releasing a passion only love could unfold

Lovers will be standing at the bar
And the valet will be parking the car
Your green eyes so bedroom soft
Would be the only thing I'll be thinking of

I'll kiss your hand as the night ends
And a dozen more roses I will send
Will you join me for dinner tomorrow night?
The ocean view is a lovely sight.

Well I hope I was able to express myself better in this poem. Call me. I wrote the number on the back of this paper.

Sincerely,

Seth Lover

She looked at the letter and smiled while Jennifer jumped around hysterically before pulling up a chair beside her co-worker. "So are you going to go?"

Veronica replied slowly, "I don't know… he's nice and all, but… I don't know." She leaned over and inhaled the fresh aroma of the roses.

Jennifer gave her a puzzled look. Her moment of silence was followed by, "Are you insane? My man don't send shit for me," an amusing smile covered Veronica's face at her friend's sudden outburst, "Girl, I think you should give that brother a call."

"I'll think about it." She picked up the bouquet and smelled them on her way out.

"You'd better call that man!" Jennifer called to her as she left.

She made her way through the store, followed by all eyes, before exiting to her car.

Ring!! Ring!! Ring!! Ring!!

"Hello?" Seth answered. He was in his office reading a book when the phone rang.

"Hello, Seth." He heard Veronica's voice on the other end.

"Hello, Veronica. How are you doing?" A wide smile covered his face at the sound of her voice, but he could not help thinking about Nikkia.

"Thanks for the flowers, but I'll have to decline from that date at this time." Her tone sounded nervous to him, like it was very difficult for her to tell him no.

"Maybe another time," he replied. He felt his heart plummet into his stomach while his body felt as though a thousand heavyweight champion boxers beat on him when they were in their prime. Her words rushed through his mind like a monsoon, thrashing every fiber of his brain, every thought.

"I'm just not interested in anyone at this time." She continued tearing his flesh off his body and burning his paradise with her words as he listened in silence. "Seth, are you still there?" Her sweet voice taunted the very viscera of his being.

"Yes___ I'm still here," he replied—his voice crumbled into his big toe.

"Say something." Her plea was not inspiring to him.

"I really don't know what to say except that if I have offended you that you would find it in your heart to forgive me."

"You didn't offend me… and what you did was sweet. The timing is just off at this time." She went on to explain as he listened in silence.

"I understand Veronica; maybe another time." He did his best to assure her, knowing he was crushed by her rejection.

"My girlfriends wanted to kill me when I told them that I was not ready to go out with you." Her sign of relief did little for him, but he was glad that her anxiety was lifted.

"You did what you felt was the best thing to do," he comforted, trying to ignore the pain in his heart as it smashed against his ribcage.

"Well, I have to go now. Sorry again, Seth."

"May I keep in touch?" he quickly asked.

"Sure, silly. Bye."

"Good night… Veronica," he replied before hanging up the phone.

He stared at the ceiling for a long time. After awhile, he picked up the phone and dialed a number. The phone rang for a few minutes before someone answered. "Hey, Mikey, sorry to disturb you."

"What's up Seth?"

"What's Veronica's last name?"

"It's Lee."

"Thanks man." He hung up the phone and continued to stare at the ceiling in thought.

Nineteen

Seth sat staring at his computer, trying to deal with the hand just dealt to him as tears filled his eyes and rolled down his cheeks into his lap. He sluggishly turned on his computer and waited for it to boot up as her words re-echoed off his being, playing images in his mind of him being beaten into a pulp by bandits. Destructive images flooded his mind one after another, twisting into him like a Samurai's sword. The desktop popped up, distracting his self-pity, so he opened his program and started typing:

My Villain

I've conquered death for a cause
To fulfill a dream and did not pause
As I served through time as servant and slave
Missing the calling of my grave

I was in love with her with all my heart
And I'm still crying since we were blown apart
As loneliness crept into my bed
And on my sorrow it fed

Nikkia, my heart yearns for your love
As you look down at me from up above

I saw a sign of God's promise to me
But she said no. How could this be?

I will face this villain and conquer it agáin
No matter the cost or the pain
And I hope in my heart I could win her to me
So I can, once again, be set free

Her voice reminds me of the love we had
Through the good and the bad
And her eyes of emeralds dancing in the night
Seem to comfort and protect against my plight

She carries the ring I was told to seek
And she reminds me of you when she speaks
Time has changed with each passing year
With my freedom seeming almost near

I felt at home in her arms as I danced her around
She's like my fountain of youth I have found
She is the part I need to make me whole
She is my reason for being in this world

As loneliness and strife try to keep me down
I will stay focused, for her heart is where I'm bound

She is the freedom I've been waiting for
And she is finally knocking at my door

I'll take my time, and hope for the best
As I plot to vanquish my distress
I hope I could find a way, for her love I must win
To end this curse I must bare for the crime of my sin

My villain is intangible and hard to beat
But I must take a stand to defeat
Time, sorrow, loneliness, and strife
For she will be my cure as my wife

He looked at his rambling, then saved it before turning his attention on his next course of action.

Twenty

Months passed, and every day that Veronica worked, Seth stopped by the donut shop and bought a donut, and chatted briefly with her. Then, on the way out, he threw the donut in the trash or took it home where it got hard. He finished his second book and was waiting for a copy to arrive in the mail. He picked up his laptop and started writing when the doorbell rang, so he went to the door to see Cindy standing there. "What's up, Cindy?"

"Not much." She entered when he opened the door. "You told me that you would be getting your book today, so I stopped by to see it."

"It hasn't arrived yet." He sat back in an easy chair with his computer while Cindy went to the kitchen.

"Tonya'll be stopping by soon; she went to get some food!" she shouted as she filled a glass with water.

"Great, I hope she brings enough for all of us!" He started typing:

Just For You

As months went by, you were always near
In my mind: my thoughts, I must declare
But though you're near, you are still far away
As night seems to be, when next to day—

"What you writing?" Cindy asked, coming over.

"I'm writing a poem." She looked over his shoulder as he continued, dancing his fingers across the keys, pouring out his heart:

—My work is done as I thought of you
An intoxicating feeling—much like brew
Not knowing if this step would hurt
I must take this chance even if it costs my shirt

Two-dozen roses I have sent
A tribute to a time done spent
With you on my mind in all I do
So I sent these flowers just for you

He looked up at Cindy and asked with a smile, "What do you think?" She looked at it for a few seconds. "You don't think it's too mushy, do ya?"

"No, it's fine, Seth." She patted him on the shoulders and leaned in closer. "So, who's it for?"

He printed a copy and picked it up answering, "It's for Veronica___ I'm going over to the flower shop and have them send it to her house."

"I hope she knows how lucky she is. Are you two dating yet?"

"Not yet, but I'm working on it."

She laughed. "A million women in America want a piece of you, and here you are chasing that girl."

She picked up his fan mail and showed it to him, but he replied, "Of all the women in this world from the beginning of time to the end, she is the only one I want."

"That's touching Seth___ I hope you get lucky." She laughed again at the remark then followed up, "You know what I mean."

"So, you coming for a ride?" he asked as he opened the door.

"Sure___ let's go." She grabbed her purse while he wrote a note on a paper and stuck it to the door stating that they will be back shortly.

Half an hour later, Seth and Cindy returned to meet Tonya sitting on the porch. "Hi, Tonya," Cindy greeted, coming up the steps, "You've been waiting long?" Seth came up behind her.

"No, I just got here about ten minutes ago." She handed Seth a package. "FedEx brought this by about five minutes ago."

"The book is here," he stated. He opened the door quickly and held it open for them to enter, and then closed it behind him.

While Seth and Cindy sat in the living room,Tonya made her way to the kitchen saying, "I'm hungry."

"Open it Seth___ I want to see it," she stated ecstatically. She sat impatiently trying to reach for the package.

"Hold on, hold on. Wait till Tonya comes back." He held the package away from her laughing at her impatience.

"Hey, Tonya, get your butt in here now!" Cindy shouted.

"I'm coming!" She jogged into the room with her face stuffed with food. Seth opened the package to reveal a black, hardcover book with gold lettering that read: *Passion Within: Heaven's Bliss.*

"It looks great," Tonya complimented as she took it from him and flipped through the pages, careful not to get any grease on it.

"That's the classic version___ The publisher is putting out that version as well as the paper-back version. They should hit the bookstores in a few months."

"That's great, Seth," Cindy stated, taking the book from Tonya's greasy fingers.

"Thanks, guys." He was happy to finally see this copy and hoped more copies of this book would sell than the previous collection of poetry.

"So, did the first one do well?" Tonya asked.

"It made enough that I made my initial investment back. But the publisher did this one, so I did not have to put out another ten thousand dollars." The doorbell rang. He walked over and opened the door.

"Waz up!" Michael shouted, "Did I get here in time?"

"You just missed it___ We opened the package already," Seth replied while Michael hugged Cindy and Tonya. Seth was grateful for Michael's relentless efforts in helping him sell his first book by word of mouth.

"How's the real world treating you?" Cindy asked as they returned to the living room.

"Not too bad, I finally landed a job down at T.J. teaching History," he replied, resting his bag on the ground.

"Where is Cathy?" Seth asked, coming back into the room.

"Oh, she had to work, so I told her good___ that way I could pickup a few lines from your new book before she sees it." They laughed at the irony since he used some of the poems from the first book.

"So where is it?" He looked around before Cindy handed it to him. He examined the cover, and then flipped through it. "I see you mixed in a few poems in this___ sweet." He handed the book to Seth saying, "When it comes out I'll get a copy, but in the mean time," he reached into his bag and pulled out a bottle of champagne, "Let's celebrate." He made his way to the kitchen followed by his friends in a chatter of noise.

"Something smells good up in here." Michael inhaled a deep breath, rubbing his stomach.

"That's my food," Tonya stated, just remembering she left it in the microwave.

"You better save a brother some of that, 'cause I'm hungry."

"Open the bottle white boy, and don't worry about my food."

"You ain't change nothing since I was here last, huh Seth?" Michael asked as he opened the cabinet and took down some glasses, "I guess not." Michael was working at the library for a few months after his graduation on a full time basis, and he did not have time to come and help Seth around the house.

He popped the cap and quickly poured the frothy beverage into the glasses while Cindy brought some ice from the freezer. "Here's to Seth and his new book, may he make some loot to take us on a cruise," Michael toasted, raising his glass.

"Cheers!" They all knocked their glasses together.

"I'll drink to that," Seth stated and took a sip. His face changed from a smile to one of disgust. “How do y’all drink that stuff?” They all laughed at his expression and distaste for the beverage.

“You never had champagne before?” Tonya asked as she took her food from the microwave.

“No, wine is the only thing I like___ wine and Kahlúa.” He grabbed a bucket of ice cream from the freezer. “Mikey___ toss me a spoon.” He quickly opened the bucket before taking the spoon.

“I think we all need to dive in that bucket,” Cindy commented, grabbing a spoon.

Michael took out a knife and fork and sat down beside Tonya, digging some of her food and stuffing it in his face as he sampled the ice cream. “Them damn kids sure work up a mean appetite.”

“Hey, I thought school was out for the summer.” Tonya stated, looking at Michael and then to the others.

“Yes, but you should know this___ since you passed most of your classes there___ a little something called summer school.” Michael always found a way to tease Tonya, who always fires back.

“Boy, I’m a hurt you.” Seth and Cindy always got a kick out of their playful taunts and knew that Michael’s quick wit always gave him the advantage.

“Stop swallowing my food.” She dug in along side him.

“You two deserve each other.” Cindy commented as she stuffed a spoonful of ice-cream in her mouth.

“I tried Cindy, but she couldn’t handle this high quality cream with her coffee."

"Y'all are wild," Seth interjected as he scooped up another spoonful.

"So you like the job Mikey?" Tonya asked, looking at him.

"For now, but I wont really know till the school year starts. But for now, it's cool," he scooped up some more of her food, "It pays the bills." He noticed Tonya was eating the ice cream instead of the food. "You eating any more of this?"

"Knock yourself out."

"Good." He started stuffing his face.

"There's some leftover Chinese food in the fridge if you want that too," Seth pointed out.

"This is good enough___ Tonya took care of me."

They ate in brief silence when Michael said between mouthfuls of food, "Hey, Seth, that money you gave me came in handy___ my car broke down and with the trade-in and that money, plus what Cathy gave me___ we were able to buy a used car. Thanks man."

"Not a problem Mikey, that is what friends are for. Tonya and Cindy threw in their share each to make up that thousand."

"Thanks y'all," he replied, leaning his head against Tonya.

"Well you deserved it Mikey___ for all the odd jobs you did for us over the years." Cindy added.

"I was happy when you decided to go back to school and actually stayed and finished," Tonya teased. "I guess I'm next."

"Y'all are like family to me___ I probably would be still working at the library if it wasn't for y'all___ especially Tonya here," Michael said nudging her. "I would still be at the library." Michael was affectionate to her, because her life was so hard, so she always found time to encourage him to stay in school to the point of pestering.

"And we will still be here if you need us too," Seth added.

"At least Seth will; he's the rich one," Tonya teased.

They chatted for a few hours before parting for the night, but Seth held Michael back. "Can I talk to you for a second, Mikey?"

"Sure thing, Seth, what's up?"

Twenty-one

"How are you and Cathy making out?" Seth asked as Michael sat down in the dining room.

"To tell you the truth, we are doing okay for now___ till Cathy goes back to school that is. After that, we'll have to see."

"What is your rent like now?"

"Well, it's six hundred a month now. Then there are utilities plus my student loan I'm paying off___ All that have Cathy and I on a serious budget. That's why I was glad you, Cindy, and Tonya gave me that ends."

Seth took a deep breath, then exhaled saying, "I don't know if this will work, but God has blessed me more than you know. So, if it will make life a little easier on you guys, this place is big enough that you and Cathy could move here," Michael listened intently, almost shocked at Seth's offer, "You would be close to work and could walk there while Cathy uses the car to go to school. The rent here will be three hundred including utilities, that way you could save some money since you are now starting out." He looked at Michael's blank expression and continued, "What do you think about that?"

"That would be a great help; I'll talk it over with Cathy tonight."

"Aside from the rent, both of y'all will have to chip in with the house work___ like cleaning in here and the yard too. Since you graduated, I had to hire a lawn service."

"That sounds fair to me." He stood, shook his friend's hand, and then headed for the door with Seth behind him.

"Do you still have that maid come over?"

"Yes."

"That was a dumb question___ of course you do." He paused and turned. "Are you sure you're twenty six? Because you act a lot older." Seth laughed as he locked the door behind his friend.

The next day Seth sat on his porch reading his book. His water stood on the table in front of him, and beside it was his cordless phone.

"Look at this horrible statement." He criticized the way he worded a situation in his book and was ready to kick himself.

Neighborhood children ran across the yards playing catch with their dogs, while others rode on the sidewalk as their assorted guardians sat on their steps, porches, and lawn chairs watching intently and catching some rays. Seth took a sip of water and continued beating himself up when the phone rang.

"Hello," he answered, putting down the book.

"Hi, Seth, it's Veronica." Her sweet voice caused a sudden rush of blood to bombard his heart as his smile widened.

"Hello, Veronica, how are you?" he said, now sitting up straight in the chair.

"I'm doing great; thanks for the flowers."

"I ain't know how you could refuse a brother like that; you brood over that damn poem he sent months ago all the blasted time," came LaWanda's voice in the background as she argued with Veronica.

"Shut up, he could probably hear you!" Veronica shouted, doing a poor job of muffling the sound. "Sorry about that, Seth."

"Not a problem." He was pleased to hear that she loved his poem but pretended not to have heard LaWanda's kind revelation. "How have you been?"

"I've been great___ Mikey told me you finished your book."

"Yes, but I'm glad you called."

"You are? Why is that?"

"Well… I have this party___ more of a gathering to go to… and you are the only single woman I know who might accompany me."

"Oh, so that is why you sent those flowers." Her pleasant voice took him back to Rome—under the tree—and he remembered the birds that sang above his and Nikkia's heads.

"Did it work?" There was a pause. His heart raced in anticipation of her answer.

"I guess so."

"Then that's why I sent the flowers," he teased. He was happy at her response and wanted to start dancing, but he thought twice about that since people were within sight.

"So when is this gathering?"

"It's Saturday night."

"And what is the dress code?"

"It's formal." He adjusted his position in the chair with a smile so wide that his eyes were barely open.

"Damn___ I'll have to go looking for an evening gown tomorrow because I'll be busy for the rest of the week," she muttered to herself.

"If you like, I could pay for it." He was glad that she accepted and was ready to do whatever it took to make her comfortable.

"No thanks, I'll manage on my own."

"Well, would you mind if I accompany you? I know this place on Cary Street that sells formal wear."

"Sure, we could do that."

"What time should I pick you up?"

"Say around one___ I'm off tomorrow, but I have some laundry to do in the morning."

"Well… see you tomorrow." He hung up the phone.

Twenty-two

Seth woke up the next morning and had his breakfast before leaving for the gym for his usual morning workout. After his workout, he drove into Cary-town, stopped at an almost empty formalwear store, and entered. He approached the counter where a middle-aged woman sat going over some paper work. Seth greeted, "Good day, Miss."

"Yes, may I help you?" the woman replied with a smile.

"I would like to setup an account here___ who do I need to speak to in order to do so?"

"You can talk to me; I'm the owner, Mrs. Malary." Her motherly smile and attention caught Seth's attention since he did not have that luxury as a child.

"Ah, yes… the name of the store," he stated, remembering the sign out front.

"You will need a show your driver's license, a second form of I.D., and a credit card to do so."

"May I write a check to establish the account as a down payment per say?" he asked, handing her the initial requirements, "I hate owing people."

"I know what you mean; I'm still paying off for this place," she replied with a grin. "Sure, honey, you could do that."

He pulled out his checkbook and started writing; then he handed it to her after making a record. "Here you go, Mrs. Malary."

"Thanks, dear." She took the check and looked at it. "Wait a minute___ Are you Seth Lover, the poet?" She looked at him inquisitively.

"Yes, Ma'am, that's me; I didn't think many people would recognize my name."

"My husband and I support local talent___ He uses some of your work when he wants to butter me up so he could go blow money," she joked as she continued filling out the paperwork.

"Does it work?" He leaned against the counter, smiling with an interest in knowing how his work affected others.

"It does sometimes, but at other times I just let him feel he's getting away with something. My daughter loves your poetry though." He chuckled at her almost comical motions that seemed similar to that of Michael. "Where are you from? I hear an accent," pointing to different locations on the documents for him to sign.

"I came to this country about seven years ago from Trinidad, an island in the Caribbean," he replied as he finished signing the papers. "I'll be bringing a friend over this afternoon to purchase a dress. She insists on paying herself, so if you could___ Do you think you could charge her a cheap price and put the rest on my account? I don't want her to find out or she'll kill me."

"Sure, I can do that." She handed back his cards and took the signed documents.

"Well, I'll see you this evening."

"See you later, dear." She started fiddling with a dress that she had on the counter beside her.

Seth came to a halt in front of Veronica's dwelling and climbed out of his car, making his way to the door. He rang the bell and stood back for a few seconds before Sandy opened it with a smile. "Hi. Seth, right?" She stuttered, hoping she said his name correctly.

"Yes, that's it, Sandy."

"Come in. Veronica's out back practicing her karate."

He followed her to the back yard and whispered to Sandy not to alert her yet. She shrugged her shoulders and went back inside, leaving him on the back steps. He sat down, watching her movements in the similar style like his own, when she turned to see him and stopped and smiled. "Hey, Seth, you're early."

"I know." She came over to where he sat.

"How long were you sitting there?"

"I just got here___ Say, you do that form a lot more graceful than I do," he replied as he stood and repeated the form. She watched him move through the form swiftly and joined in at the middle, synchronizing with his movements. Sandy saw them and came out smiling as they finished and came over exhausted.

"Hey, Veronica, I thought not too many people knew that form?"

"So did I. Where did you learn it, Seth?"

"From an old Chinese master some time ago, but I've been out of practice."

"You did a great job at it. You need to stretch out a little, but it looked great." They made there way inside. "I learned it from my father." She hurried down the hallway saying, "I'll be right out."

"I see y'all finished packing," Seth observed as he sat down.

"Yes, we finally did last week," Sandy replied, handing him some water.

"Thanks." He was grateful that she offered him the water because he did not realize how thirsty he was until he started drinking it. He did not gulp it down though, because his manners would not allow him.

"Where's LaWanda?"

"Oh, she went to work; she won't be back till later." Sandy was bustling around the kitchen, putting stuff away. "So what y'all have planned for this afternoon?" she asked, leaving the kitchen and taking a seat opposite him after she finished her cleaning.

"She's going to buy a dress for a party I have to attend this Saturday."

He finished the water when she leaned in and whispered, "I think she likes you. She's been going on about that poem you gave her some months ago, but she's a little scared." She looked to see if Veronica was coming then added, "You didn't hear that from me, okay?"

He smiled. "Okay."

She took the empty glass into the kitchen and then came back and sat down saying, "Mikey told us that you finished your second book."

"Yes___ That party we're going to this Saturday is held by some people in the publishing world___ That's why I'm glad Veronica is going, so she could hold off those___ how do you call it? ___Yes… groupies, who attend those gatherings."

"So what is this book like? Is it another collection of poetry?" She leaned back in the chair and crossed her legs.

"It's a romance novel, but I mixed in some poetry in there too."

"It sounds nice. When does it come out in the bookstore?"

"In a few months."

Veronica came down the hall. "Sorry for keeping you waiting, but I had to take a quick shower." She flipped her hair back and pulled it into a ponytail, then tucked her T-shirt into her jeans. "You ready, Seth?"

"Yes." He stood and made his way to the door as she followed. He held the door open for Veronica and said to Sandy. "See you later."

"See ya." She came up to close the door while Seth caught up to Veronica and opened the car door for her.

He, once again, pulled into *Malary's Formal Wear's* parking lot and parked his car in front of the store. Then he quickly jumped out to open the door for Veronica before following her into the store. Mrs. Malary came over while a sales woman attended to her customer saying, "Come in, how may I help you?" Her pretence of not knowing Seth was flawless.

"I'm looking for an evening gown for this Saturday___something inexpensive but still great-looking but isn't too fancy looking," Veronica replied as Seth took a seat in a corner next to the changing rooms.

"Come this way. We have a great variety," Mrs. Malary informed decisively as she selected one, "This would look great on you; not too many people could wear this." She leaned into Veronica and whispered her thought, "Because some women are all chest and no butt." Veronica chuckled at the joke, and they continued selecting more clothes.

"We'll find a few that you like; then, when you select the one you like best, I'll measure for any needed alterations. Then I could give you a price___ So don't fret over the prices now, okay dear?" Mrs. Malary insisted motherly as she scurried around the store, suggesting selections for Veronica.

"I think this is enough," Veronica stated under a pile of clothes.

"Okay, dear, go and start trying them on," Mrs. Malary, holding open a changing room door for Veronica.

She tried on every dress and modeled them all for Seth and Mrs. Malary, who thought they looked great on her. But in the end she settled on an Oriental style, armless silk dress with an open back. It hugged her body from her neck to her waist; then it flowed freely off her buttocks, complimented by two slits up the side of her legs.

"Oh dear, we'll have to hem this up, but other than that, it's a perfect fit. How do you feel in it, dear?" Mrs. Malary started sticking a few pins in the dress and marking where the alterations needed to be made.

"It feels great." Seth eyes almost fell from their sockets when she modeled, and he thought she looked great in her decided attire. His silence was rewarding. She would glance at him with a smile as though looking for approval. Her dimples always caught his attention, and he yearned to caress them.

"Good, now go take it off," Mrs. Malary ordered in a motherly tone when she finished marking the dress. Veronica spun, glancing at Seth as she made her way back to the dressing room. She came out a few minutes later carrying the dress while the other sales person returned the remaining dresses to the racks.

"So how much is it?" Veronica asked as she came up to the counter.

Mrs. Malary fiddled with the calculator as she mumbled to herself, then looked up and replied, "That will be one fifty. It is on sale."

Veronica reached into her pocketbook and paid for it saying, "That's great. I even have enough to buy a pair of shoes tomorrow."

Mrs. Malary gave her the receipt with the change. "It will be ready for pickup tomorrow afternoon dear."

"Great___ I can get it after work." She turned to Seth. "Come on Seth, let's go."

He stood and stretched as she left the store. "Hey, Seth, we pulled it off___ the other part of the receipt will be mailed to you tomorrow," Mrs. Malary whispered.

"Thanks Mrs. Malary." He headed for the door and exited.

He opened the car door for her and then suggested after spotting a restaurant across the street, "Hey, Veronica, let's grab a bite to eat across the street at that Indian restaurant there."

"Okay." She sauntered beside him after he shut the door and started walking to the sidewalk.

"That was fun," she expressed after a moment.

"What was?" They crossed the street when it was safe to do so.

"Trying on all those dresses of course," she propounded, looking up at him.

"Whatever works for you, Veronica." He was thrilled to be with her, but tried to be cool. He was doing a good job at it, but he felt awkward not being himself in that respect. He held the door for her and entered behind her.

They entered the restaurant and were seated, and after ordering the food, they sat in silence for a moment.

"So, Veronica… tell me something about yourself," Seth finally said. She smiled.

"Like what?"

"Like the things that interest you… what you like to do for fun… those kind of things." He took a sip of water.

"Well, I like working out. I love poetry, dancing, and music. I love sitting in an open field___ probably under a tree just feeling the breeze blowing around me, then looking up at the bright stars___ which incidentally aren't so bright around here." He pictured Nikkia sitting under the tree out in the meadow looking up at the stars in the early night as he wrote on a napkin. "What are you writing?"

"You'll see for yourself just as soon as I'm done; I need to capture this moment." He finished and handed it to her with a smile. She took it and started to read silently:

A Gorgeous Image

The dim lights capture your dazzling eyes
With a gentle flare to my surprise
In a restaurant room so cozy and small

As soft music plays of a lover's call

You closed your eyes and trusted me
Releasing your charms: making them free
Enchantment dancing all around you
A radiant display seen by a few

Roses picked and boxed as a gift
I wish I had for you as I started to drift
You opened your eyes with your dimples revealed
A lonely soul is once again healed

Lunch is served as we chat for a while
But what held my attention was your lovely smile
That showered blessings only I could see
A gorgeous image created just for me

"Since you like poetry, I thought you might like that." He was all smiles as he absorbed her favorable expressions.

She looked at it then at him and smiled. "You just thought this up?"

"Yes, you inspire me whenever you're near," he replied as the waiter served the food.

"You are very talented." She fell silent and shook her head, as though spellbound, with flushed cheeks. Her slight smile of approval revealed her dimples that excited him, but he was bashful to say so.

"What am I going to do with you?" She spoke to herself, holding back all her secrets that he wished she would share. But her immediate reaction said it best, and she did not need to reveal anymore.

They ate in silence as she admired the poem with a smile and an occasional glance at him as he pretended that he did not see her green eyes illuminating under the dim over-head lights. After eating in silence, he looked up and asked, "You ready for dessert?"

"Oh no, I'm good." He signaled for the check to be brought to him, as she reached into her pocketbook.

"I got this, Veronica."

"Well at least let me pick up the tip," she demanded. He smiled.

"Go for it." Her independent nature impressed him to know that she was selfless and willing to carry her own weight. He paid for the meal as she placed the tip on the table before leaving.

Seth communicated with Veronica, much to his delight, most of the week. They met in the evenings in her back yard where they practiced their martial arts form together. He felt happy for the first time in over two millenniums, standing next to her, observing her smile as she occasionally pulled her long hair away from her face, engulfing a warm feeling around his body. He embraced her gentle taps whenever he teased her or whenever they fell against each other in practice. The world remained oblivious in her presence where nothing mattered—but her. That Friday, he bade her farewell until he returned the next day for the party.

Twenty-three

He pulled onto his street and parked behind Michael's car. Then he jumped out and climbed the steps to the porch where Michael and Cathy stood to greet him. "What's up, guys?" He shook hands with Michael and then gave Cathy a hug.

"Not much. We decided to take you up on your offer," Michael replied.

"So where is your stuff?" he asked, looking around.

"It's in the car," Cathy informed as Seth opened the door and locked it into place so it remained widely open.

"Okay, let's get your stuff."

They started making trips from the car to the room. After about half an hour of moving in, Michael paused to inhale deep breaths. "Here is the first month's rent." He huffed from the exhausting trips as he handed a check to Seth.

"Thanks, the rest of this month is free, so this will cover next month." He slid it into his pocket. "Do y'all have anything else to bring up?"

"Just a few things, but we could handle it," Cathy replied, wiping the sweat off her face with her forearm.

"I'll be downstairs if you need me," Seth informed as he descended the steps, then turned, reaching into his pocket and tossing his key to Michael saying, "Make a copy and give that back; I can't seem to find my spare."

"Sure thing Seth, and thanks for helping us out."

"Not a problem. You guys are my family." He continued down the steps and entered his office.

Cathy came down a few minutes later on the way out the door, but she stopped when Seth called out, "Hey, Cathy, I forgot to tell you___ There is a phone line running to that room. All you have to do is activate it."

"Okay, Seth, we'll do that on Monday," she replied, shutting the front door behind her. Michael came down a few seconds later and went out to the porch to Cathy as Seth gazed out into the back yard at the pine trees dancing in the hot breeze. His thoughts wandered to Veronica as he sat looking out while the setting sun was casting red and orange rays across the sky. He reminisced on her smile, her laugh, her touch, and her voice as he turned on his laptop and waited for it to boot up. A few birds flew by and landed on the bird-feeder, then they dashed off again, putting a smile on his face as he turned back to the screen and started typing his thoughts:

Happiness Is She

Time played its game so well
Each passing moment—a living hell
But I endured, and soon freedom is at hand

Like the passing waves across loose sand

Happiness seems to be here

Whenever she's near

A blessing sent from up above

Sent with God's love

Emotions from a time long past

Are returning to me at last

A future with her is what I see

Because___ happiness is she

He saved it and then joined the others on the porch.

"I'm running down to the store to have the keys cut. Do you need anything, Seth?" Michael asked him as he sat down next to Cathy.

"No thanks," he replied, throwing his arm around Cathy's neck.

"Okay, I'll be back." He slinked his lanky body down the steps and drove off.

"So, how's life treating you?" Seth asked, turning to Cathy.

"It's great, and now we don't have that high rent over our heads, I think we'll do fine___ At least now I could concentrate on graduating next year." He could see that a weight was lifted from her and was glad in that respect that he was able to help.

"Thanks again for offering a place here till we get on our feet."

"Don't sweat it; like I said, y'all are my family." He gave her a comforting squeeze.

Seth woke up late the next morning, showered and changed, and then went downstairs. He bumped into Cathy as he turned to enter the dining room. They both jumped back, startling each other, and then broke out laughing.

"You startled me, I forgot y'all was here," Seth commented with a smile, falling on her neck.

"I didn't here you coming down," she stated, punching him playfully on his arm.

"Man… you still sleep late." Michael observed, brooding over a stack of papers.

"I stayed up late reading," he walked over to where Michael sat, "What you doing, Mikey?"

"Just grading these papers," Seth sat down beside him, "I'd forgotten how comfortable these dining room chairs were."

"Hey, Seth, you want some breakfast?" Cathy asked, making her way into the kitchen. "I bought some groceries this morning___ since your refrigerator was empty___ except for that spoilt milk and dry bread." She often teased him in the past about his refrigerator, and this time was no exception.

"What you talking about___ I have peanut butter, mustard, ketchup, and some other things in there," he answered back. He always tried to justify it but knew he could do better at stocking it. "I was going down to Aunt Sarah's, but if you insist, sure I'll have breakfast."

"Damn… I'll have to give this kid's mother a call. There has to be a way to help him pass these tests," Michael muttered under his breath.

"Wow, I thought you hated children," Seth stated, leaning back in the chair. Over the years, Michael had a low tolerance for children: more of a fear for being responsible for them and their safety.

"They're alright; I guess I'm growing a soft spot for them."

"What's the problem?"

"This kid really shows interest; it must be the tests," Michael stated, shaking his head, "If he fails this class, he'll get held back another year."

"Maybe he's more of an oral person. Try asking him to talk about what he learned. It might work," Seth suggested, remembering his lessons with Titus's children.

"Of course, I didn't think about that. Thanks, Seth." Cathy brought in the food.

"Thanks, Cathy." He was happy to get the home-cooked meal since he had been alone for so long. They chatted for a few minutes before parting company to accomplish their daily errands.

Twenty-four

Later that evening, Seth strolled down the steps in a sporty suit and made his way to the kitchen. He came back to the front door holding a rose, checked himself in the mirror one last time, and then he exited the house. He pulled an envelope from his pocket and attached it to the rose as he jumped into his car and rested it on the seat beside him. His smile covered most of his face from the moment he came down the steps till he pulled up to Veronica's house. He placed the rose on the dash; then he jumped out and made his way to the door, adjusted his clothes, and calmed his excitement before ringing the bell. Then he waited for a few seconds. Veronica opened the door dressed in her evening attire with a smile.

"Hi, Seth. Let's go."

"Hold on, hold on a minute… can't a brother admire you for a second?" he teased, looking her up and down and exaggerating his motion. She smiled and spun around, holding her purse closely.

"Okay, now we can go," he stated, taking her hand after she locked the door. He opened the car-door and helped her in under the setting sun that shone brightly off the triple-wax job done previously that day. Then he climbed in behind the wheel.

"Thanks for the rose, Seth," she stated, taking it off the dash.

"That isn't for you." He tried to keep a straight face as she quickly put it back.

"Sorry."

He laughed at her embarrassed frustration and could not hold out any longer than a few seconds. "I'm only teasing; it's yours."

She punched him on the shoulder as he started the car, threatening playfully, "I'm ah hurt you Seth." She took the rose and removed the card, and then opened it and started reading after smelling the flower:

I'm Blessed

It's good to know you're at my side
As I pull from your house in my sporty ride
Time could stop for all I care
Because you're next to me my dear

Down the street—I'm taking my time
Enjoying this moment so sublime
I'm on top of the world thanks to you
From the top of my head to the dirt on my shoe

This long road ahead is all to see
God knows I'm glad you're next to me
An oblivious world as I change gear
Reminds me that we just met last year

I'm blessed to know your name
I'm blessed if you feel the same

I'm blessed 'cause you are here

I'm blessed because of you my dear.

A smile covered her face as she held the card looking at it when he broke her thought.

"You look stunning this evening; I was caught up in the moment and forgot to mention it earlier."

"Thanks, Seth," she replied smelling the rose again, then looking down at the poem.

He glanced over at her and noticed a strange expression on her face. "Is everything okay? What's the matter?"

She smiled and looked at him replying, "I'm fine. You say some of the nicest things in your poems. Do you mean them, or is it talent?"

"It's a little bit of talent, but every word is true___ I have no reason to lie about my feelings." But he was nervous that her reaction might have been a negative one and was still unsure of her thoughts. He did not pry though; instead, he decided to wait to see what would happen next.

People stood around conversing and sipping on champagne or martinis, dressed in tuxedoes and fine evening dresses. Seth was ushered in with Veronica on his arm as heads turned to see them. A woman in her fifties excused herself from a conversation and came over to greet them. "Seth, darling, I'm glad you could make it." She greeted him with a hug, then turned to Veronica and asked, "Who is this lovely lady?"

"This is Veronica; Veronica, meet Mrs. Viniski. She graciously gave me an opportunity to have my work published."

"Please to meet you, Mrs. Viniski."

"Oh, Seth is quite the charmer; he charmed me with a poem and got me hooked," Mrs. Viniski teased as she grabbed Veronica's hand, "Go mingle, Seth. There are a lot of people here who read your book and are dying to meet you—especially their wives." She walked away, pulling Veronica with her.

"Don't take her too far!" he called out as she gestured for him to mingle.

He walked through the crowd meeting different people who wanted to discuss his book and possible rights to use his work for music.

"Hello, Seth," a beautiful woman came up to him and greeted.

"Good evening," he responded, shaking her hand.

"I'm Claire Davenport; I believe you met my husband earlier."

"Ah yes___ the music producer," remembering the black man with the fat diamond on his hand.

"Well, I bought a copy of your poems and found them intensely erotic. That's quite a talent you have." She grabbed a glass of wine from a passing butler. "Would you like a drink?"

"Thanks, I do what I can when I write… and no___ I have to drive a special young lady home tonight, so I'm not drinking."

"Suit yourself." She took his hand and pulled him along, "Follow me, I want to introduce you to some women dying to meet you." He looked around for Veronica and saw her talking to some men with Mrs.

Viniski on the other side of the dance floor when a young man came up and took her for a dance.

"Seth, this is Tina, Rose, and Jennifer," Claire informed, introducing him to the ladies. They looked to be in their mid thirties with a youthful spunk about them, but he focused on Rose.

"Don't you workout at the same gym as I?" He did not find her attractive even though she had a killer body and outgoing personality. And now he felt even stronger about this feeling since Veronica was his focus of attention.

She recognized him and replied, "Yes, you are usually leaving when I'm getting there." He shook her hand. "What a small world we live in."

"Seth, I read a copy of your new book… it is fabulous," Tina stated. She was of Oriental descent and had an exotic look that he noticed. Her beauty did not distract him, although in another time, he would have been tempted to embrace all that is she.

"Thanks, I did not know it was out yet." He glanced over to see Veronica dancing with Mr. Viniski but was careful not to offend the women's company.

"I did the editing on the book for publication," she informed with an inviting smile. He spoke with them for a few minutes then excused himself, taking a glass of wine and strolling over to where Veronica sat after her dance.

"Sorry I got pulled away," he apologized, giving her the wine, "Are you having a good time?" He was concerned that he was not spending enough time with her and hoped she understood that it was not his intention to leave her among strangers.

"I am. Mr. Viniski and his son were really nice. So was Mrs. Viniski___ but my feet are killing me in these shoes." She took a sip of the wine as he stooped down, slid off her shoe, and started rubbing it.

"How does that feel? He looked up into her eyes, and she smiled. His passion for her was growing with every touch, every smile. The image of Nikkia was still present with every word she spoke, which made him more careful. He was afraid that he might call her Nikkia like he did with Cindy some time back.

"It feels great, but stop… those women over there are giving me an evil look. I don't think they like me very much." He gently slid the shoe back onto her foot and took off the other saying, after taking a glance in the direction she indicated, "Don't let them bother you. My concern is only you." He rubbed her foot and slid the shoe on then stood, saying with a smile, "Now save a dance for me."

"I will." She looked up with a smile as Mrs. Viniski came up to them fussing.

"Seth___ go mingle___ most of these people will be selling that last book of yours, and you need to leave a good impression," she fussed and hustled him to mingle with a gentle push, "Your beauty will still be here when you come back," she teased him at the same time.

"Okay, Mrs. Viniski." He looked down at Veronica smiling, then turned and started mingling again.

Twenty-five

An hour or so later, Seth looked around for Veronica and saw her with Rose at the bar, so he strolled over and apologized, "Forgive the interruption, but I believe I've kept my date waiting far too long."

Rose looked up from her stool. "Don't worry, honey, I kept her company."

He looked at Veronica longingly, "If it's not too late, may I have this dance?" She took his outstretched hand, and he guided her to the floor, locking eyes—once again—as he took her in his arms, feeling her delicate touch around his neck, enjoying her warmth.

"Sorry, I did not expect this tonight… I was wrong to leave you among strangers."

"Don't worry. I was a little jealous that all the ladies wanted you, but aside from that, everyone was nice."

He smiled, holding her closely and wrapping his arms around her waist saying soothingly, "I'm glad you're here with me. Thank-you."

They danced slowly around the dance-floor, gazing into each other's eyes as the music seemed to spin around them, engulfing them in a room to themselves. He looked into her eyes, admiring the green coloration and then at her beautiful face as she smiled at him with her intoxicating dimples. He could feel her breath against his face and her long hair between his fingers as he lost all thought of everything but her. Her warm body pressed against his, distracting him as she leaned in slowly, gently resting her lips against his neck. The sensation flooded through his body like a rushing wave. She then pressed her lips against his; he tasted the wine from her tongue and her warm lips that softly entwined with his. His heart raced in his chest as they parted from the unexpected kiss, brushing their cheeks together. He held her tightly not knowing what to do next, just waiting for the song to end. His mind focused on the moment, remembering the feeling of an almost forgotten sensation as he felt her hands on his back, caressing his tense muscles. The song finally came to an end as he stood there looking into her smiling face, searching to see where reality ended and fantasy began. She smiled at him—a blank expression possessed his face—he was still holding her closely.

"Seth… the song is over," she informed, patting him on his face and brushing her nose against his.

He smiled and replied as he guided her off the floor. "Yes…it is___ I could have sworn you kissed me back there."

She smiled, holding his hand in hers. "I got caught up in the moment."

Seth jumped into the car after closing Veronica's door and started the engine. A cloud floated above, waiting to explode as the wind blew across the estate. He could feel every organ in his stomach twisting to the sudden change of events as he started the car and looked over at Veronica's smiling face while she fastened her seatbelt.

"Thanks for the lovely evening, Seth." He started driving down the driveway onto the street.

"You're welcome." His thoughts were fragmented, but his body had a sudden burst of energy, something that was long forgotten.

"You really made me feel special tonight, and those women only added to the fire knowing that they wanted you and I had you." She reached out and took his hand as it trembled under her touch with excitement. He quickly squeezed her hand in an effort to cover his excitement as he glanced across at her. He fought the tears of joy as he felt her warm hand in his—he, inhaling the fragrance she wore. His sight, his touch, his movement, his hearing, and his sense of smell seemed to be in overdrive, picking up every detail from her all the way to her door. He climbed out and helped her out; then he walked with her to the door as the rain drizzled down on them.

"Don't forget your rose." He held up the flower with the card and handed them to her.

They paused at the door for a moment, and she looked up at him saying as she wrapped her hands around his neck, "I really like you, Seth. Somewhere between Mikey's graduation party and lunch the other day, but tonight only harnessed that feeling that finally over-flowed."

He looked into her eyes as his hands circled her waist saying, "From the moment I picked you up for Mikey's party and you placed that chain with the ring on it around your neck, I was in love with you." She reached up as he reached down, locking lips and holding each other closely, tasting her as his heart raced in his chest, his body saying, "*Don't let go*," but his spirit saying, *"Take your time."*

He broke the passionate kiss that awoke dormant desires, and she opened the door saying, “Good night, Seth.”

“Good night.” He took her hand, lifted it to his lips, and kissed it, gazing into her bedroom eyes, wishing he could stay but knowing he should leave. He turned and strolled to his car, not thinking about the now pouring rain. He heard her door close, then open, and he turned to see her running back to him. He caught her in his arms as she kissed him again.

“I love you, Seth.” She dashed back into the house. He climbed into his car and drove home, aching with emotions as they flooded through his body.

He opened the door, quickly changed his clothes, and then came down and turned on his computer. The rain pounded against the window while he waited for the computer to boot up. He opened a program and started typing as his mind replayed the evening’s event:

A Storm of Love

We walked to her door without a sound
As the drizzling rain came pouring down
Arm in arm in romantic bliss
She reached across and gave me a kiss

She entered her house—soaking wet
As I started thinking about a bassinet
I looked to the sky to find the moon
While my head felt inflated—like a balloon

The streets looked gloomy in the rain
As she ran outside and kissed me agáin
Soaking wet, but we didn't care
Me, thinking of marriage then and there

I could have never dreamt of a time so dark
That love could have found me with just a spark
There was beauty in that storm tonight
When she said she loved me and held me tight.

He saved the poem and then turned off the computer and went to bed, thanking God before humming himself to sleep.

Twenty-six

Several months passed, and school re-opened for the fall. Veronica and Seth met whenever they could, but when their schedules conflicted, they would chat for hours on the phone. On the weekends, they usually spent the evenings in Seth's den watching movies or taking long drives in the picturesque countryside of Goochland. One Friday night while watching a movie, Michael and Cathy came down on their way out.

"Hey guys, we're going out!"

"Have fun!" Veronica called back. The door closed, and she leaned back against Seth in his lazy-boy chair, drinking ice-tea and eating popcorn. She reached up, putting some popcorn in his mouth as he held her closely.

"Man, my legs are killing me this week," she exaggerated, propping her foot up and rubbing them. He took the popcorn from her hands and set it down while shifting his body and standing to his feet. He disappearing for a few minutes and then returned with a container of warm water, setting it before her.

"What are you doing?" She looked down at the water. He removed her socks without a word and then gently eased her feet into the soothing water.

"I'm going to solve that little problem with your feet," he finally informed with a smile as he left again and returned with a bottle of baby oil and a towel. He sat down on the floor in front of her as she looked down at him, smiling. He slid the container to one side and wrapped her feet in the towel before resting them on his crossed legs. He poured the oil in his hands and started rubbing her foot, stretching the ankle in all directions, before massaging the sole and between the toes. She watched him from behind those green eyes, smiling as he concentrated on her foot—before slowly massaging her calve.

"That feels great." She leaned back in the comfortable chair as he gently massaged her muscled leg and then switched to the next foot. His hands glided over her leg with the aid of the oil, releasing the muscle tension as she closed her eyes, relaxing under his touch.

"Does that feel better?" he asked, standing to his feet and picking up the container of water.

"That was great, hon.." She stretched her hands over her head. He took the container into the kitchen. He returned and lifted her into his arms before sitting down again with her across his lap as she smiled at him, giving him a kiss and resting her head against his chest.

After a moment of silence, she asked, "When did you learn to massage like that, poet?"

His muscles tensed when the familiar nickname left her lips. He looked down at her, asking as he searched her face, "Nikkia?"

He tried to get up, but she said, "Don't move Romelus, I've waited a long time to be in your arms and enjoyed the past few months in this position."

"When?" he inquired intently, holding her closely, "Tell me everything." This new revelation shocked him. He was both confused and ecstatic as he squeezed her in his arms.

She smiled as she took a deep breath and then said, “I’ve had dreams most of my life of when we lived in Rome___ before you left___ but I always viewed them as dreams,” he started caressing her hair, “But I was scared when I first saw you because you looked like the man in my dreams.”

“Is that why you did not go out with me that time I asked you?” He squeezed her again.

“Yes. The uncanny resemblance shook me, but the dreams started to come more clearly, which made me curious.”

“I see.”

“That night I kissed you at that party we went to at Mrs. Viniski’s, I had fallen in love with Seth, but after that kiss, all the memories flooded my mind and by the time you took me home, I was sure.”

“Was that why you ran back out and kissed me?” He kissed her cheek.

“Yes, I wanted to tell you, but I was not sure how you would react. Plus I wanted to see if you had changed over the years.”

“How did Father do it?” He kissed her neck as she played with his hair. His smile was wide, and tears rolled down his face.

“He sent me back when this body got conceived, mentioning something about a covenant to fulfill with you,” she wiped his tears as he did the same for her, “So what do you think about this new body?”

“You look great___ different___ but great,” he replied, squeezing her again and nestling his face on her shoulder.

"Nikkia, Nikkia, Nikkia." He kissed her cheek and then her eyes, nose, and lips.

"My name is Veronica now although I reserve the right to still call you Romelus, poet, or Seth."

He lifted her in his arms as he stood, spinning around shouting happily, "No more Titus, just you and me!"

"Stop! You're getting me dizzy!" Her laughter refreshed him with new zeal as he spun her around before setting her down.

"You haven't changed much since you took me to Heaven," she observed as she ran her fingers through his hair, "You know, the long hair look has been out for a long time. Don't you think you need a haircut?"

"Anything for you, Veronica." She was teasing, but he took it literally and made plans to get a haircut as soon as possible.

She looked into his eyes and asked before kissing his neck, "Do you still have those wings?" Her whisper had new meaning that seemed to overwhelm him. He looked at her smiling face, touched her dimples, and then guided her to the back yard.

"I can only do it one more time before I lose my immortality; Father told me I'd be able to transform one more time as a sign that his covenant is complete with me." They stood in the backyard, engulfed by a gentle breeze. "Let's see if it is done."

His hair changed to gold as his body, once again, became covered in armor that bonded with is body. Power surged through his muscles as his wings shot from his back and opened, lifting him into the air. His eyes changed to gold once again as he looked around,, seeing angels surrounding them. He smiled and reached out for her. "I've waited a long time to take you flying." He lifted her into his arms, and she wrapped her arms tightly around his neck while he held her firmly around her waist. He kissed her as they ascended above the clouds before parting from the lip-lock.

"Don't look down." She looked down and let out a scream as she held on tightly.

"Don't you drop me, Romelus." He could feel her hands holding him in a death-grip.

"Why would I do such a thing after I waited thousands of years for this moment," and held her a little tighter so she may not be as scared of the height. "I can feel your touch in this armor, but it is not the same without it. Once we descend, God's gift will leave me, and we could finally grow old together."

"Let's go home." She, touching the hard armor, before reaching up and kissing him, "I don't like the feel of this armor either."

A flash of light approached and stopped before them like a mirror image of Seth. "Our Father's covenant is complete," Richard greeted.

"He looks like you," Veronica stated, observing their company.

"I am Love. Thanks to Romelus's faith in our Father, I exist today."

"Good luck my ancestor, I am glad we were allowed to meet." Richard shook Seth's hand before disappearing into the night.

"Is he your descendant?" she asked as they floated before the moon.

"Yes, I had a child with a Roman a few days after your marriage to Titus when I got drunk at his party; it was God who told me about the child I had and his plan for my seed."

"Look at that moon___ After all these years, you kept your promise to me," she stated, leaning against him as they looked at it. "Now that I'm with you, you don't have to do that anymore."

"After I showed Titus the *Fear of God*, I came to the moon's surface and wrote, '*I love you Nikkia; may our love meet in another time.*' I wish you could see it." They descended to Earth—she, loving him all the more that he did that daring feat for her. He knew the lack of atmosphere would kill her, and he could not protect her from death and was saddened that he could not show her the inscription of his love for her.

The cool air blew through their hair as they descended, his angelic figure slowly disappearing as his feet touched the ground, holding her firmly in his arms. He felt a chill across his back as she pulled away from him saying and blushing, "Seth, you're naked."

"The armor does that," and he hurried into the house. He made his way upstairs, put on some clothes, and came back down. "These clothes are different from the togas."

She looked at him, complaining, "The movie ended and we didn't even see it."

"We could always rewind it___ I'm just glad to be with you." He took her in his arms again.

"I really want to stay, but I have to get up early to go to work," she replied, kissing him and patting his chest.

"What time do you get off?"

"I'll be home around one." He walked her to the door and down to her car, not wanting her to go but knowing she had to.

"I'll see you tomorrow." He kissed her for a long time, until she unwillingly pulled away. He stood there till she disappeared around the corner.

Twenty-seven

The next day Seth woke up early and disappeared down the street to the barbershop. The cool air brushed against his face as he strolled down to Lafayette Street and entered the small barbershop there. The owner greeted him at the door. "Morning, what'll it be?"

"Good morning, sir. I want a short fade." The elderly gentleman seated him. Seth watched his hair fall to the ground and wondered if this was a mistake, but the barber worked skillfully with his scissors and clippers, cutting his hair with almost zero at the sides and back, fading up, leaving about three inches at the top. He spun Seth around to face the mirror and then he dusted the hair off his neck before removing the covering from around him.

"That's a lot different look, son. You look like a soldier now. What do you think?"

Seth ran his hand over his head and replied, "I'll have to get use to it, but it looks good." He stood to his feet and paid for the cut, and then made his way home. Cathy saw him coming up the steps to the porch but did not recognize him at first.

"May I help you?" she inquired and then smiled, realizing who he was. "Seth, you look great. Why the sudden change?" She came over and ran her hand on his head. "Euw, I got hair on my hand." She tried to rub it off on her pants.

"Veronica thought I'd look good like this, so I took a chance." He opened the door but stopped and turned back to her. "Where's Mikey?"

"He's out back___ about to do the lawn."

"I'm going up and take a shower. I have some things to do today," he stated, before he stepped into the house. He came down sometime later and jumped into his car, disappearing down the street.

A few hours later, he pulled into the donut shop's parking lot and looked at the time.

"Almost twelve thirty." He looked up at the sky through his glass top. Veronica came out a few minutes later, running over to the car as he climbed out to greet her.

"Hey, Seth, I was on my way over. I missed you last night." She jumped into his arms, wrapping her legs around him and kissing him.

"You look great with that hair cut, but I didn't think you were going the do it," playing with the two earrings on his ear as she brushed his head with her free hand.

"I am glad you like it." He squeezed her and seated her on the hood of his car. He looked up at the sky at a plane flying by and smiled as a cloud of smoke emitted from its rear. He looked into her eyes as he brushed her dimples. "I've waited a long time for this," and pointed to the sky as the plane maneuvered around, forming words.

"A sky-writer, I didn't think they did that anymore!" she exclaimed.

"I thought so too until today."

"What's it saying?" she asked herself as he stepped back from her taking something from his pocket. She strained her neck looking up reading as the plane formed words.

She read: "Ve…r…o…ni…ca… Le…e, will… you… ma…rr…y me…? … Se…th." She smiled as she looked back at him. He was kneeling before her opening a ring box, exposing a ten-carat diamond engagement ring.

"From the moment I saw you in Titus's garden all those years ago, I've waited for this moment. Veronica Lee___ will you marry me?" Tears rolled down her cheeks as she looked at him and at the sky, before jumping off the car and hugging him against her stomach as she sobbed.

"I've waited a long time___ hoping for a chance to hear those words from your lips___ from the day you comforted me in the garden till now." A crowd of passers-by looked up at the sky and then across at them.

"Does that mean yes?" She took his face in her hands and lifted him up, sobbing.

"Yes, poet, yes___ I will marry you." He smiled as he slipped the ring on her finger.

"I hope it fits, I had that made a long time ago." They hugged and kissed. He grabbed a radio in his hands and spoke into it. "She said yes."

"Who are you talking to?" she asked, still holding on to him as she dried her tears. He pointed up again as the plane wrote the words against the sky. *She said yes. Congratulations.* She laughed as they read the words while passers-by smiled and couples held each other tighter on their afternoon walk. He kissed her again, finally finding peace in his heart—he stroked her hair.

Spring came around again and Seth and the newly weds, Michael and Cathy, sat at the dining room table.

"What's up, guys?" Seth asked as he looked from Cathy to Mikey, who smiled widely.

"We just put a down payment on a small house out in Henrico," Michael informed.

"That's great." He was shocked at the news but was glad to know that they were standing on their own in such a short time.

"We still have a shit-load of bills that we're paying off slowly, but we managed to save enough for the down-payment and closing costs," he added.

Cathy came over and stroked Michael's head stating, "And since I'll be graduating in a few months and already have a job lined up, we thought it would be a great time to move."

"So how much is the house?" Seth was still a little concerned that they might be extending their means.

"It's sixty thousand. I got a thirty year mortgage with the bank I'm with," Michael replied.

"I'm proud of you, Mikey. I'm glad you didn't blow all your money like you did when we worked at the library."

"I have responsibilities now; besides, my mother didn't work like a dog so I could go to school and let her down like that."

"And we had you to advise us too, Seth," Cathy added.

"When do y'all move in?" he asked as he stood.

"After I finish finals," Cathy replied ecstatically. She did well in school, despite her struggle with work and her class schedule.

"Excuse me for a second," Seth stated, and he disappeared into his office and returned a few minutes later. "Did y'all settle yet?"

"Yes, we did yesterday," Michael replied as Seth sat back down, "We gave the people till Cathy's graduation in two months to leave."

"Then we'll move in and slowly furnish the place with the money I'll be making," Cathy added.

"Great, here is a check: it's the rent you paid me with a little extra as a home warming gift. I was waiting to see when you two were going to deserve this, and I believe that time is now."

"Thanks, man," Michael replied, taking the check. He was grateful for the money that he knew would come in handy when they moved.

"You were saving our rent?" Cathy asked, looking at it. She knew Seth was a generous man, and although he was not much older than they were, she felt protected by his brotherly love.

"Yes, I only used that rent thing as an excuse to make sure y'all had some money," he replied as she came over and kissed him.

"Thanks, Seth."

Twenty-eight

"Are you nervous?" Michael asked Seth as Seth put on his suit. Michael and Cathy had already moved into their house, but he came over to take Seth to his wedding.

"I've waited for this for a long time, but hell yeah, I'm nervous." Michael hooked Seth's comma-band.

"Here, put on the jacket, and let's go," Michael hustled him. They were not late, but he did not want to take the chance.

"Do you have the ring?" Seth asked, throwing on the jacket and checking himself in the mirror.

"Seth, I'm glad you're getting married, but women change once you say I do," Michael teased as he pat his friend on his back, showing him the ring, and making their way down the steps.

Seth ran into the kitchen as Michael called from the front door. "Hurry up, Seth. We need to get going."

"Okay, okay, I'm coming." He came back to the front, tucking a red rose into the jacket collar. "Here's the keys." He tossed his car-keys to Mikey. They made their way to the car and Michael climbed behind the wheel and adjusted the seat and mirrors.

"I've been waiting to drive this baby for awhile." Seth sat down beside him.

"Don't let the power go to your head." He knew Michael would be careful but could not resist the temptation to tease him.

"Me and this car was made for each other, so don't worry."

He started up the engine, threw it into gear, and pulled off, stalling immediately.

“Like a glove,” Seth remarked, buckling the seatbelt.

“I just got to get the hang of it,” Michael assured as he fired up the engine again. He was not use to driving stick since his car was an automatic. He punched the accelerator, riding the clutch. The tires burned against the asphalt as he pulled from the curb.

“My car!” Seth shouted out in concern, looking over at Michael.

Michael laughed—hysterically shouting, “The power, I can feel the power.” He stopped at the corner and then burned the tires as he pulled out onto Malvern, gaining control once he put the car into second gear.

The car skidded with better control onto the street where the church stood as Michael parked and jumped out.

“You are crazy___ How did you pass your driving test?” Seth teased as he shut the door. He remembered doing the same thing when he first bought it and was not upset at Michael.

“That was great,” Michael stated with exhilaration as he looked over at Seth. “I got you here in one piece, didn't I?” He threw his arm around Seth's neck and pulled him into the church.

“Hey, Cindy, glad you could make it,” Seth greeted as he gave her a hug.

“I wouldn't have missed this for the world, Seth. Congratulations,” she replied as Mikey hugged them both.

"Where's Tonya?" Seth asked, looking around before spotting her at the front of the church. "Tonya!" he called out, waving his hand. "Excuse me, Cindy." He made his way to Tonya.

"Hey, boo, congratulations," she greeted, giving him a hug.

"Mom, you look as young as me," he teased as she adjusted his clothes and tie. She was playing the role of mother giver today, which he was grateful for.

"Well someone had to be the mother giver," she stated, "How do you feel?"

"I am a little nervous___ hoping nothing will go wrong." He looked around the church at the people coming in. "Where's Tom?" seeing Robby sitting at the back of the church.

"Cindy and him broke up last week." Seth had not seen Cindy in about two months with all the preparation for the wedding. It saddened him that this bad luck befell her.

"This looks like a one-sided turn-out," she commented, looking at all Veronica's family and friends with a few friends of Seth's scattered throughout the church.

"I'm sure my folks are looking down from Heaven." He saw Stephanie and waved at her.

"They're getting started, Seth," Michael informed, coming up to them and taking his position. Seth waved at Veronica's mother, who came up front, as the Preacher approached the pulpit. The music started playing as he looked back to see Veronica, escorted by her father, walking down the aisle towards them. Her dress glittered against the overhead lights, flowing about ten feet behind her, with her golden veil covering her face as she held a bouquet of flowers in her hand.

Michael leaned over to Seth and whispered, "How much did you spend on that dress?"

"A lot."

Tonya smacked Michael behind his head and pinched Seth. "Behave you two." They smiled at her and stood silently. His heart raced faster the closer she got, as a feeling of joy overwhelmed him. Seth smiled wider when her father handed her to him—he took her arm, positioning himself beside her before the Minister and waiting for him to begin.

"Dearly beloved, we are gathered together to witness the joining of Seth Anthony Lover to Veronica Ashley Lee in holy matrimony," the Minister addressed the crowd, "If anyone wants to speak out against this union, now's the time to run your mouth." He looked around as the crowd chuckled. "Since no one said anything, if any of you have anything to say after the wedding condemning these two people, take it up with God." They chuckled again as the Minister turned his attention to Veronica and Seth. "Are either of you having doubts about this?"

"No." They responded in unity.

"Okay, Seth, look at Veronica and repeat after me. I Seth take you Veronica to be my lawfully wedded wife." He repeated the words. "To love, cherish, and honor." He repeated them, with his hands trembling in hers, so she squeezed them. "In sickness and in health…" He repeated the words till the end before turning back to the Minister with a smile.

"I saw you shaking in your boots," the Minister teased. The

congregation chuckled as Veronica took his hands and repeated the words to Seth.

"The rings," the Minister requested, looking at Michael as he nervously fished them from his pocket.

"Thanks, son." He took the rings from him. He gave one to Seth saying, "Put this on her finger and say, *with this ring I thee wed*." Cathy helped Veronica remove her glove before Seth slid the ring on, repeating the Minister's instructions. Veronica did the same before facing the Minister together with Seth. Seth squeezed his fingers together, adjusting the ring as he held Veronica in his arm. The Minister looked to Veronica's father and asked, "Do you give this woman to this man?"

He stepped forward. "I do." He stepped back as the Minister looked to Tonya and asked the same question.

She stepped forward answering, "I do," and then she stepped back with a smile.

The Minister leaned into Seth and Veronica teasing, "Seth, your mother's young; your family must age well." They smiled at the joke as the Minister straightened up and looked at them, saying in a loud voice, "With the power given to me by the state of Virginia, I now pronounce you husband and wife." Seth quickly raised her veil, but the Minister stopped him. "Slow your roll, son. You have the rest of your lives for that." They laughed as he continued addressing the crowd, "Let no man come between what God has joined together." He looked at Seth, "You may kiss your bride."

Seth lifted the veil over her face, gazing into her green eyes then down to her smiling dimples. He pulled her to him, and their lips locked. He dipped her then lifted her into his arms shouting, "My wife!"

The congregation stood as he set her down and escorted her down the aisle under a shower of rice.

"A toast to the bride and groom!" Michael announced, grabbing a microphone. "Since I'm the best man, I was given the honor to say a few words." He looked at Seth and Veronica and then to the crowd that filled up the rented hall. "Seth and I are about the same age, but he got money and I don't." The crowd laughed. He looked at Seth. "But you had me worried for a while there, Seth; I thought you were the hermit from the hood because no one ever saw you with a girl until Veronica came along." He looked at Veronica. "And as for you, Veronica; although you were hunted down, chased, and cornered by many guys, you held out strong for this rich one." He paused, looking around before he addressed them again saying, "I've had the privilege to know both of you, and I must say that the two of you deserve each other. I'm glad that I met my wife so you could have met each other; good luck my friends." He lifted his glass and took a sip, followed suit by the bride and groom, and the roomful of guests.

"Mikey, you think we could cut the cake now?" Seth asked, leaning over to his friend.

"Let's do that," he agreed, making the announcement as they stood and made their way to the cake. Veronica had already taken off the bottom part of the wedding dress, transforming it into an evening gown. The cake stood three layers tall, with flowers and fountains leading up a flight of stairs to a miniature couple at the top. They cut the cake and served each other, and then they shared some champagne, twisting their faces in reaction to the unpleasant taste. Cathy handed them some juice to cover the taste as the crowd around them laughed at the scene.

"Alright, guys, time for your wedding song," Michael instructed, directing them to the dance-floor while the DJ popped on the selected tune as they held each other.

"*Moments In Love, by Arts of Noise*, because there are no words to describe how you make me feel," Seth whispered in her ear as the music started playing.

"I know what you mean." Their eyes met as they smiled, enjoying the song and holding each other tightly.

"I can finally call you my wife." She smiled at him.

"Yes, our love finally met in this time," she proclaimed. The song came to an end, and they left for their honeymoon, finally finding peace in each other's arms.

Part Four
Poems Dedicated To You

Of all the people in this world

You were the one who read my work

And I thank you for your support

By leaving you with my last thought

Happy Circus

Dancing bears at the circus show
And funny clowns on their horns did blow
With hearts around, skipping beats
When performers do their daring feats

My heart skipped once or twice
But it was not for the performing mice
It was the sight of you next to me
Because you are the only performance I wanted to see

Your graceful dance put the bears to shame
And your gleeful laugh could tame
The lions jumping through hoops of wire
As well as my soul trapped by fire

I am happy in this scene we sat
Among all around in some funny hats
I'm standing above from once below
You alone: I love you so.

Beach Completed

You're standing on a beach of ivory sands
Bordered by blue-green water from God's hands
While silver clouds formed over you
The sun seemed bright shining through

Your hair flows gently in the salty breeze
While your brilliant smile seem to tease
Passers-by as they strain their necks
To look at you on their lonely treks

I watch you look out to sea
Then slowly turn and smile at me
I finally know why the sun shines bright:
Your smile is a gorgeous sight

Your bedazzling eyes seem to search my soul
But in them I do behold
A sparkle of many flickering stars
Under the sound of instrumental jazz

You perfect the scene before me
So in my heart I must decree
That I learn of you in every way

To be mine by Saint Valentine's Day

My World

The trees of green standing high
With a river slowly slithering by
While the birds sing their happy song
As I look at you for so long

The majestic mountains in the distance
Are an enchanting sight for instance
Yet I see in this creation
The source of my inspiration

It is you, with your perfect smile
That can keep me blushing for a while
And your gentle touch so heaven sent
Seems warmer than the inside of o'r tent

The dusty path became suddenly calm
As the dancing trees attempt to charm
Yet it is you, my dear, I'm glad to meet
For it is you who make my world complete.

Heaven's Gate

The golden stairs was a long wait

As it led up to the pearly gate

Silver clouds along the sides

Flowing wings on my divine guides

As I neared the gate, there you stood

So I hastened my pace as best I could

Although Heaven's gate was elegant and tall

I enjoyed—more—the sound of your call

I'm in your arms as the serpents hissed

And saw Heaven's gate when we kissed

Heaven is being next to you

As we strolled along through the zoo

I Love You

The sun was shining bright

And the music was playing just right

With all the neighbors out having fun

On yard work just begun

You joined me outside, with drink in hand
And in the other, a silk fan
With a beautiful smile always present
Adding to an atmosphere so pleasant

You reached out your hand and gave me a drink
As a neighbor waved from his outside sink
Barbecue chicken from a house down
Spread an aroma all around

Summer was near, with spring coming to an end
Standing beside you: my lover and friend
I am lucky, this I swear
I am in your arms, your loving care

Honey, I love you with all of me
With a love that will last an eternity
I'll remember this day when you quenched my thirst
For you are my last, as you were my first.

Hello Lady (Part One)

Hello lady; take my hand
Music's playing by a live band

The atmosphere is mellow for this dance

As I wanted you from my first glance

Let our bodies join on the dance floor

Let's enjoy each other; let our hearts soar

Look into my eyes and see my soul

Release your passion—let love unfold

Lovers are standing at the bar

And the valet already parked your car

Your captivating eyes so bedroom soft

Hold my attention and love

I'll kiss your hand as the night ends

And a dozen roses I will send

Will you dine with me tomorrow night?

Because the ocean view is a lovely sight.

Hello Lady (Part Two)

The ocean breeze was blowing slow

Against the flickering candles and their gentle glow

This private room shared a view

Of the ocean below and the sunset too

You entered the room in an evening dress
And a diamond pendant on your chest
Hello lady—you look great
Thanks for accepting this date

As we ate together, o'r eyes met
Admiring your orbs against your jewel set
But they could not match your bejeweled smile
As you looked at the birds as they flew by

Under the setting sun you learnt of me
I hoped you'd fall for me by this sea
As we kissed goodnight before we part
You took with you, my only heart

Your car came around in the valet's care
Brightening your face as your stared
At your car covered in flowers:
A sight I could watch for hours.

Nothing Without You

I am with you, a lovely lady
Take my hand to this Spanish melody

Gracing the scene in complete elegance
With the night full with romance

Your warm body close to me
Lifts my spirit to set me free
While people dance all around
And others stand just looking on

Your soft breathe across my ear
As light reflects off the chandelier
Our cheeks brushing as we move
To a melody so smooth

I feel like I'm standing in another world
With a lifelong story not yet unfold
Our eyes lock, then o'r lips
In o'r world of an eternal trip

Darling, may this night last forever
And that we don't part, never
You were part of me from the start
I'll be nothing without you if I break your heart.

Secret Admirer

Fluffy clouds of ivory white
Cover the sky and Heaven's light
As snowflakes cling to the icy slopes
Making it safely is what you hope

Your graceful motion cuts through the snow
As I wait for you down below
An admirer for who you are
When I see you sitting across the bar

I just want you to know that I'm attracted to you
Just as much as the ocean's blue
Will you join me for dinner in the lodge?
Enjoying a sundae smothered in fudge

This is a letter of my feelings for you
I don't mean to offend; that's not what I want to do
I am your secret admirer
Who's interested in who you are.

Dream Night

With fear in our eyes like in a ferocious storm
We stepped on the ice in amateur form
Not knowing what to do as we tried to skate
But being with you was my good fate

We moved around as slowly as can be
As I fell twice like spray in the sea
Laughter and music was constantly there
While a cool breeze blew through your golden hair

Around and around, getting better each time
Brought back memories to this rhyme
Two hot chocolates as we started to leave
My God lives in Heaven, which I now believe

We walked to the car enjoying the night
As we chat of a distant future bright
I'll remember this night as it comes to an end
The night I spent with you my friend

Mountain View

On a mountain we stand looking down
At the sight below and the echoing sound
Of your voice of laughter over the trees
Sweeter that the honey from the honey bees

You sing my name like a nightingale
As you put on polish on your fingernail
The trees dance in the gentle breeze
With one intention: that's to please

The mountain view is dazzling
Yet I see something more amazing
All the beauty that I could see
Prove you to be the most beautiful to me.

Hello Dear

Hello dear; how are you?
I'm still out to sea with my crew
At first chance, I'll mail this letter
But getting home to you would be better

The nights are bright and full of stars

And I could sometimes see the planet Mars

While the waves constantly rock my boat

But there is nothing here for me to gloat

The whales sometimes swim real' close

Yet my mind seems to be on you the most

And dolphins pass from time to time

Adding color to this little rhyme

We are almost done with this job here

So I'll hurry home to you my dear

The ocean is lovely and quite blue

But I'd rather be home next to you.

Home At Last

Snowflakes are falling all around

As I trek on homeward bound

Chilling wind across my face

Inspire me to hasten my pace

Up ahead is my home

So, that is why I fail to roam

You see me through the windowpane
And rush outside as though insane

Nothing, but your bathrobe on
And our baby yet unborn
My face glows at sight of you
As you pull me close knowing what you want to do

We walked on together through the door
Me, loving you all the more
So slowly time did pass
I'm in your arms: I'm home at last

About the Author

Milan, 27, is a college student at Towson University. He served in the Marine Corp. and then worked in a corporate environment. He currently attends Towson University studying English, Writing Concentration. He believes that if we embrace the power that love provides and share a smile with others, we could conquer all odds.

Printed in the United States
1394600001B/172-195